The Secret Habit of Sorrow

The Secret Habit of Sorrow

Stories

Victoria Patterson

Counterpoint
Berkeley, California

THE SECRET HABIT OF SORROW

First paperback edition: 2018

This book is a work of fiction. Names, characters, places, and incidents
are the product of the author's imagination or are used fictitiously.
Any resemblance to actual events is unintended and entirely
coincidental.

Grateful acknowledgment is made to reprint the following:
Robert Creeley, "The End of the Day" from *The Collected Poems
of Robert Creeley 1945–1975*. Copyright © 1962 by Robert Creeley.
Reprinted with the permission of The Permissions Company, Inc., on
behalf of the Estate of Robert Creeley.

Library of Congress Cataloging-in-Publication Data
Names: Patterson, Victoria, author.
Title: The secret habit of sorrow : stories / Victoria Patterson.
Description: Berkeley, CA : Counterpoint Press, [2018]
Identifiers: LCCN 2017058815 | ISBN 9781640090521 (softcover)
Classification: LCC PS3616.A886 A6 2018 | DDC 813/.6—dc23
LC record available at https://lccn.loc.gov/2017058815

Jacket designed by Nicole Caputo
Book designed by Wah-Ming Chang

COUNTERPOINT
2560 Ninth Street, Suite 318
Berkeley, CA 94710
www.counterpointpress.com

Printed in the United States of America
Distributed by Publishers Group West

10 9 8 7 6 5 4 3 2 1

For Cole and Ry

The End of the Day

Oh who is
so cosy with
despair and
all, they will

not come,
rejuvenated, to
the last spectacle
of the day. Look!

The sun is
sinking, now
it's
gone. Night,

good and sweet
night, good
night, good, good
night, has come.

ROBERT CREELEY

CONTENTS

The Secret Habit of Sorrow

How to Lose

Natalie woke that morning with blood between her thighs and dripping down her legs. Usually she can predict her periods, but her body's out of whack from the abandoned fertility treatments. AJ wants her to watch him practice holding his breath in the bathtub, so she sits on the toilet lid. He wears his blue swim trunks. "It feels good," he says, stepping in. "Not too hot," he adds, reminding Natalie that he's better off—at eight—filling the bathtub and gauging the temperature himself. He closes his eyes, holds his breath, and slides below the water, legs still bent in the short tub, his hands fisted at his sides. She watches his eyes open and widen.

A second later he's sitting up, shaking his dark wet hair, saying, "I opened my eyes underwater!" Plugging his nose with thumb and forefinger this time, he descends again, cheeks air-puffed, eyes squeezed shut. She feels him counting, practicing, determined. One of her long brown hairs is stuck tentacle-like to the tile near the faucet. At least he's bathing and his hygiene has improved. She remembers the time she'd gone to take a shower and noticed a foul odor. Then she'd found a mixing bowl from the kitchen full of his urine. When she'd asked why he'd peed in the bowl and left it by the toilet, he'd said, "I just wanted to."

Bad Luck Thursday, AJ calls today, because his swim lessons are on Thursdays after school. He's the only one in his class who hasn't gone underwater. This is his last chance or else he's a Guppy again, quarantined to the wading pool blowing bubbles with the toddlers. "I can't be a wuss," he told Natalie. For the past week he's been practicing holding his breath in the bathtub and counting to ten.

Glen, a kid AJ's age who lives down the street, is in the advanced swim class. Glen's mom told Natalie that Glen's "kid-needy," and AJ's welcome over any time. Natalie wants AJ to have a friend, but all AJ says about Glen is that Glen laughs too much and always has a runny nose.

The other day AJ told Natalie that he believed he was fat. They had a serious discussion. No one, AJ insisted, said this to him. No one at school, not Glen, not Glen's mom. He'd figured it out by looking at Glen's body when they were changing into swim trunks and then comparing it with his own. Natalie told AJ that he wasn't fat and that, in fact, he was on the lean side. Glen was very thin and would fill out in time. At their ages, she explained, bodies changed quickly. She swore she'd let AJ know if he got fat. But later he wanted to talk again. He'd decided that she wouldn't tell him the truth.

"Why?" she asked.

"Because," he said, "you're my aunt and don't want to hurt my feelings. You feel bad already and sad for me like everyone else does." He didn't say because his mom died, but she knew that that was what he meant. AJ calls Natalie Mom in public now—he's been doing so for over a year, and living with her coming on two—so people won't talk or ask questions. But in private she's still Aunt Natalie, because they both feel an unspoken devotion to his real mother, no matter how much she fucked up.

"You're wrong," Natalie told AJ. "You can trust me. As your aunt and your legal guardian, I'm obligated to tell you if you're fat, because it's a health risk and my responsibility is to keep you healthy." This seemed to appease him.

AJ dresses and then sits for his breakfast, his usual: a toasted chocolate chip bagel with cream cheese on his favorite Sponge-Bob plastic plate and a matching pebbled plastic cup of orange juice. Natalie believes—like AJ's therapist once told her—that a busy schedule and a routine are best for grief and trauma, and she and AJ both appreciate their rituals. They've been late to school too much, and Natalie urges AJ to hurry and eat. She doesn't want to face the office ladies again, particularly Ms. Jenkins with her disdainful, crinkled powdery face. AJ's hair is damp and his cheeks flushed. She knows he's still thinking about the swim class. He leans over and pats Sugar, their tiny black mutt, who waits for scraps under the table. Sugar used to run in frenzied circles as if still caged at the pound. Now three years later she mostly sleeps—making comforting wheezy snore noises—and limps when she walks as if her front left paw is sprained, though the vet can't find anything wrong.

"Here," Natalie says, running a towel over AJ's head, and he ducks, saying, "Stop." But then he holds still and lets her dry his hair, his glance granting her permission. He picks at his bagel and takes little sips of orange juice, delaying on purpose. They both hate the school drop-off. Saying goodbye is difficult, more so lately. Does it have to do with the second anniversary of her sister's death? They've tried not saying goodbye, walking together to class, not walking together, feigned indifference, pep talks and affectionate sendoffs, hand-holding assurances, simply touching pinkies one last time in a coded I-love-you goodbye. His brave and sweet expression, how he tries not to be afraid—tries not to cry—devastates her, and most of the time she drives away from the school in tears.

In the buildup to drop-off the tension escalates, and this morning he says, "I hate school, I wish it would burn," and she says, "Eat your bagel." Her husband, Phil, a production assistant, works long hours and travels and is barely home, so he can't take over the drop-offs like the school counselor suggested. When Phil's home it's like he's an affable spectator to AJ's deep connection to her: Natalie's never had such a bond, as if she and AJ are continuously together in their thoughts.

"We need to go," she reminds AJ now, and he swipes his hand across the plate in frustration, the half-eaten bagel landing on the carpet, and then leaves for the bathroom, where she knows he'll dawdle. Sugar gets a corner of the bagel in her mouth before Natalie pulls it out.

On the drive to school, AJ apologizes and then stares out the passenger window. It's the usual blue-skied Southern California morning, a few white bushy clouds and the palm fronds shimmering.

He says, "You don't think I can do it?"

"You can," she says. "You've been practicing."

He faces her. "What if I can't?"

"Really," she says. "You've been practicing."

"A pool is harder."

"Lots of people have trouble learning to swim," she says.

"The noise under the water is different than the bath," he says. "It sounds"—he considers, then decides—"like a big empty space that can swallow me."

She's about to respond when he adds, "I hate that sound."

"The noise won't swallow you. I promise."

He gives her a patient look.

"You want to skip it?"

He looks out the window again.

"I won't be disappointed," she says, in case. She knows he knows she has a policy against quitting. "We can do private lessons."

"I don't want to be a wuss," he says.

"Please stop using that word."

They're silent for a minute.

"What if I buy earplugs? That might help. People wear them in the pool all the time."

He nods thoughtfully and she's pleased.

A minute or so later he says, "There, look!" and she sees the old Asian women who walk in a group near his school, wearing wide-brimmed sun hats, some with canes. She silently blesses the ladies, knowing AJ believes that spotting them is a good omen.

They're on time and AJ tells her not to park the car, meaning he'll get out at the drop-off on his own, she shouldn't walk with him today. He has his look—I'm going to be brave, it says, I'm trying, I'm doing my best, because I love you and need you and need you and love you—and she feels herself clenching as she pulls the car to the curb. He steps out—resolute—and gives her a grim look. There's something wizened and sad in his expression, some finality, acceptance, and incomprehension, and she feels the equivalent blooming inside her. She pulls the car from the curb and drives away, fighting the tears, knowing that he is, too. In her rearview mirror, she sees him slumped with his oversized backpack, making his way among the other kids to his room.

NATALIE'S SUPPOSED TO work on designing a website, but when she gets home from buying the earplugs, she can't concentrate. At her desk, underneath a stack of papers, she finds a form she'd filled out for AJ's baseball coach. She hadn't turned it in, instead filling out another with a more generic, more acceptable response. There's an *X* over the form, but she can still read it:

> Are there any personal or physical problems I should know (or conference privately) about?
>
> *My sister, AJ's mother, died last year of an accidental overdose. AJ found her. He said she looked like a mannequin of his mom. He*

can't look at pictures yet. Therapist says this is normal.

She was the youngest; I'm the oldest.

This morning I noticed his breath smelled and I said, "Have you been brushing your teeth?" Yes, he said, but he's brushing with water only!

I'm in over my head.

Natalie crumples the form and throws it in the trash. She liked AJ's baseball coach, with his practical, military-like sense of discipline. He wore a cumbersome metal back brace over his fancy shirts to the games and practices, and at the preliminary parent meeting, he said that though he wanted and expected to win, baseball wasn't just about winning. "It's also about learning how to lose," he said. His wife she liked less, with her long peach-colored nails and self-possessed efficiency, sitting in the stands and gossiping while slicing open her mail with a knifelike mail opener. Natalie got in the habit of waiting in her car for AJ. During the games she volunteered in the snack stand, pouring boiling water into Cup-a-Soups and making hot chocolates. AJ wanted to quit, and he purposely lost his bat, admitting he let it roll from the trunk when he was supposed to be putting it away. He also scribbled two sad faces in permanent marker on the interior of the passenger car door on their way to practice one afternoon, swearing later he hadn't, suggesting that she'd left the car door open and someone wandered over and vandalized it when she wasn't looking. She remembers how she surprised them both by yelling "Bullshit!" and that almost immediately afterward he confessed. Despite everything, they finished the season. AJ keeps his trophy on the bedstand next to his lamp.

PHIL CALLS DURING his break. "Don't worry," he says. "He'll be okay. Whether he makes it or not."

Natalie sits on the couch and puts her cell on speaker on the coffee table. She lifts Sugar and places her on her lap, smoothing her fur, Sugar's eyes slitting with pleasure. The ibuprofen she took earlier has made her menstrual cramps feel ghostly.

"He's putting too much pressure on himself," Phil continues.

"He's got the doggy paddle down," Natalie says.

"Good!"

"The other kids in his class are already younger than him. Imagine having to be a Guppy again."

They're quiet for a minute, listening to Sugar's wheezy snore.

"A month from now, he won't remember," Phil says. "It won't matter."

"I wish," says Natalie. "He says the sound underwater has an emptiness that's going to swallow him. So I bought earplugs."

"It's probably related to Gina," he says.

"Isn't everything?" Natalie says.

Phil considers for a minute and then says, "He's come a long way."

She knows he's talking about the field trip. His class had gone to the *Queen Mary*. Natalie hadn't volunteered to chaperone, thinking she'd get a break.

AJ had called from his teacher's cell phone, not sounding like himself, more like a robot.

"What is it?" she'd asked.

"I'm fine," he said, monotone. "I'm okay. I took a bus and I'm in Long Beach."

"I know you're in Long Beach."

"I'm on a field trip," he said. "I'm okay."

"Why are you calling?"

Then the teacher was on the line, asking if Natalie could please come pick AJ up, something seemed wrong. "I don't mean to scare you," the teacher explained, "but it's like he's incapacitated. He won't move. He barely speaks."

In the car on the way home AJ apologized and said he didn't remember getting to the *Queen Mary*.

NATALIE STILL TEXTS her dead sister. A one-way conversation. It's a strange habit and no one knows. After she hangs up with Phil, she texts—*I hated learning to swim. I thought about telling AJ. But it might make it worse. We had those matching red bathing suits. You had this radiance and didn't seem to care what anyone thought. I used to think, What's that like? You'd make me laugh so hard. I heard Phil describing you to a friend the other day and he said, She was alternative before the word "alternative" was a thing. I keep thinking about that*—and she presses send.

A minute or so later, her phone dings and Gina's name pops up. She doesn't look at the message, savoring the idea that her sister is alive, knowing it's crazy. But finally the anticipation makes her check: *WRONG NUMBER*.

Strangely giddy, she texts: *Who is this?*

But whoever now has her sister's number doesn't respond.

Natalie laughs—really laughs. Wrong number. Gina would love that. She's still laughing, a painful joy, as if she's her sister, too, and Sugar looks at her quizzically.

AJ REMINDS NATALIE of her sister. The way his voice grows tremulous when he turns emotional; how his upper lip and chin wobble before he cries. How he looks out the car window with that faraway expression, as if realizing something he wishes he hadn't. They've got the same thin-shaped face—mouth, eyes. His are brown; hers were blue. But they're the same, the left eyebrow swooping upward in what looks like a tiny cowlick. She decides to tell AJ, saying, "You remind me of your mom." As soon as she speaks, remorse and pity stir, and she worries that she's upset him. He's at the dining room table, picking at a peanut butter and jelly sandwich, not wanting to eat too much or too soon before swim class. Sugar is dreaming under the table, her tail *thap-thapping*.

"You remind me of her, too," AJ says.

She's surprised.

He takes a sip of his water and then asks: "Why don't you and Uncle Phil have kids?" He sees something in her face and says, "Sorry."

"It's okay," she says. "We've tried."

He nods. "I like Uncle Phil," he says, peeling the bread from his sandwich. "Mom used to say," he says, "that you were the responsible one, Aunt Caroline the ordinary one, and she—Mom—the bad one."

"Your mom always thought she was worse than she was," she says.

AJ says, "My teacher says everything happens for a reason. But I don't think so."

"That's stupid," Natalie agrees, adding, "and not true. Bad things happen for no reason." He seems uncertain, so she adds: "Your mother didn't mean to leave you."

"Okay," he says, looking away.

NATALIE SITS IN the stands and watches with the other parents and spectators. She wears her darkest sunglasses in case she gets emotional. The instructor, Emiliano, is a high school junior from the water polo team—the lessons are at the outdoor high school pool—and he takes AJ aside near the showers, sensing his nervousness, giving him a pep talk. Emiliano is handsome— he likes to look at himself and flex his muscles—and he's kind. She watches him gesturing as he speaks. AJ nods solemnly. He's wearing his earplugs, but she knows he can hear, and his swim goggles are perched on his head like glasses, kicking up his hair. Seven other students have showered and assembled in the shallow end, waiting. The water is bright and sparkly and smells of chlorine. There's a light, tickling breeze and a golden-orange afternoon glow. Natalie sees Glen's advanced class partitioned near the deep end, Glen gliding underwater like a porpoise. His mom has brought her own portable chair and reads a magazine.

Emiliano leads AJ to the steps and they wade in. Natalie feels her stomach constrict, understanding that AJ is going first while the others watch. Emiliano demonstrates floating on his back; then it's AJ's turn, and he flips to his back and floats with Emiliano's hands beneath him but not quite touching. He's doing very well. His blue swim trunks—the same ones he wore all week to practice in the bathtub—inflate a bit. The kids are in a circle around them, the water undulating in little waves. Next AJ stands and pulls his swim goggles down to cover his eyes. He grasps the side of the pool and kicks his legs, and when she sees that his face is down in the water, her chest balloons with anticipation. She loves him and will always love him and he is hers and she is his. Then he lets go of the side and submerges below the water and she counts with him: one, two, three, four— imagining the terrible sound, a pulsing nothing that swallowed her sister—and he's up again at ten. Emiliano is smiling, and AJ, she sees, has pulled off his goggles and is searching for her face. She lifts from the stands and sees him see her—his stare incredulous, his smile growing, his arm lifting, and his hand with the goggles waving. Her legs tremble as she goes to him.

Vandals

Brian's ex-wife, her new husband, and the kids were on vacation in Oahu, and Brian had agreed to water the plants and bring in their mail. Having completed these tasks, he stood at his son's bedroom window and looked out toward the field, where a man and two kids flew a kite in the unpredictable Santa Ana winds, the kite swooping and nose-diving. Their house, perched above his son's high school, had a steep incline spread with trees and foliage that led to an easily scaled fence and the football field and track below. Teenagers left behind their debris on the hill: used condoms, empty alcohol bottles and beer cans, lighters, earrings, pens, clothes, shoes.

Brian and Rachel had bought this house with Jason's future in mind. Brian still remembered how the waving palms, blooming jacarandas, and other wide-ranging flora had seemed so lush for Southern California. They'd separated when Jason was eleven; Brian had moved to a nearby condo, where he still lived. His goal had been to get Rachel back—there'd been little fighting during and after the divorce. But when she remarried, he lost hope. Teachers and other parents often praised them as a model for postdivorce success. He didn't dislike Rachel's husband and his son, now Jason's younger stepbrother, and it was easy enough for him to help out when they left town.

Brian sat at Jason's desk and opened his laptop. He knew Jason had moved on to less parent-accessible forms of social media, but he nosed around his son's open Facebook page anyway. Before he'd left on vacation, Jason had blocked a girl, Madeline Dominguez, sad-eyed with long dark hair. He scrolled their previous chats. Generic flirtations until a few days prior, with Jason commenting: *Leave me the fuck alone psycho slut.* A drab nausea formed in his chest. Jason was a sophomore. It was easy to be cruel at his age.

He found Madeline's Instagram, with her selfies posed in mundane locations: mouth open, tongue stuck out and pointed in different directions, lips scrunched, eyes wide open, eyes shut. What was she doing?

He shut the computer and then lay on Jason's bed, closing his eyes to nap. But he opened them with a sudden rush of fear. What was he doing? Why was he still here? For a long time he stared at a photograph of Jason on the side table, handsome and earnest in his football uniform, on one knee as if proposing marriage.

Then sleep came in fitful, aggressive waves with images of

Madeline puckering her lips in that ubiquitous fish pose or sticking out her tongue like Miley Cyrus, tauntingly and obnoxiously sexy. He woke, thinking of his cousin Laney, whom he hadn't thought of in years.

He'd been fond of Laney when they were children, and his parents and her parents had encouraged them, posing them in photos holding hands and kissing. Their affection escalated—seven, eight, nine years old: whispered declarations of love, furtive meetings in hideouts, partial nudity. One afternoon Laney kissed him with tongue, and they groped each other until his leg shook so violently that they both got frightened and stopped. Years later on a family camping trip, Brian snuck into Laney's tent. They became adventurous, entwining their naked bodies in her sleeping bag, thrusting, kissing, experimenting. Then a flashlight beamed down and Laney's father stood over them. As Brian gathered his clothes and dressed, Laney's father—his uncle—made them agree that whatever had happened would never go beyond them and that it had to stop. The next time he saw Laney was two years later, and her face revealed nothing, as if their past hadn't existed. A rift between families completed their separation. He'd heard that Laney had had a tumultuous time during her twenties, but who hadn't? Technically they'd been each other's firsts, though he'd never told anyone and felt sure that she hadn't as well.

Brian was supposed to meet a woman for dinner that night—their third date, an attorney like him—but he called and canceled. Before he'd moved out of the house, he'd built a pond in the backyard with Jason's help, and now he poked a stick in the water, creating ripples. The sun was down, sky darkening, the water a reflective surface, trees hanging in it, shadows developing. The back porch light timed on, and a mesh of hexagonal gold glints crossed the surface. He'd put so much time into this pond, and Rachel and Jason hadn't appreciated it. Now it was neglected, the water thick and mucky. From the corner of his eye, he thought he saw something move underwater, small and fast.

He'd tried to keep fish alive, experimenting with fat koi, dumb and pretty, who had died quickly. A great blue heron kept eating them, and when Brian had placed a net over the pond the bird impaled the fish through it.

Torpedo-shaped golden orfes lasted longer, yellow and silver at their flanks. They swam in groups and gathered under the shade, shimmying and shaking, with two or three sidled against the bubbling oxygenated air-rock as if enjoying a Jacuzzi. One morning all twenty-three died, the sickly smell creeping through the trees and bushes, past the grass, over the flowerpots, and into the house. Fine suspended particles of silt—runoff from the neighbor's yard during El Niño rainstorms—had stuck to their gills, asphyxiating them.

Brian heard a rustling. Voices, laughter. The wind stirred the leaves, and he moved to the base of the unfenced yard. Whispers, more laughter, the fiery tip of a blunt along with the skunky smell, the bluish light from a cell phone. Two teenagers.

He slid down ten feet or more with his back and butt against the hill, careful to go slow and not make noise.

The voices got closer and he moved sideways.

"I'll do the front, you the back," said a girl's voice.

Along with their defiant and determined demeanors, he intuited that they were headed to the house for some kind of revenge.

He saw the tops of their heads. The boy held the girl's elbow. When her face tilted up, Brian heard himself say, "Madeline?"

"Jesus, fuck," said the boy, and then a scurrying movement through the bushes—leaves shaking—and the boy was gone.

Madeline peered at Brian, her eyes asking: How do you know me? Who are you?

He stood frozen, heart pounding.

She leaned forward, yanked a backpack to her shoulder, and started moving away. When he could no longer see her, he heard the sound of her feet thumping against the track.

Brian decided to keep the lights off so that it would look like no one was home, sure that Madeline and her friend would eventually try again, and that this time he'd catch them. He decided to sleep in his ex's bed that night. But he grew angry and restless, twisting his body in the sheets, and he fantasized about trashing the house before Madeline and her friend got the chance, and then somehow becoming a savior, both destroyer and hero. He happened to be passing by, he'd tell Rachel and Jason, when he noticed something amiss, and then he scared the burglar off, but not without a fight. Finally he admitted that ransacking the house wasn't an option, though he might drain the pond.

He remembered how Jason as a kid would watch at the window for him. As soon as he caught sight, Jason couldn't contain himself, opening the front door and running down the walkway, a soft little eager body, so that Brian was afraid he'd fall—and one time he did fall—and Brian would say, "Slow down, be careful. Be careful!" He'd kneel to Jason's height and spread his arms, and Jason would hurl against him.

Time had passed and his relationship with his son had changed—faded—as Jason became part of this other family, with Brian on the outside.

Rachel and Jason had moved on long ago, he decided, while the slow drag of years had worn him down in a prolonged disintegration. He longed then for Jason's small body as a kid, and the physical intimacy of touching, kissing, hugging.

The next morning Brian made scrambled eggs with chives and cheddar, toast with butter and blackberry jam, and after he'd eaten, washed and dried the dishes, and put them back where they belonged in his ex's kitchen, he decided to call his son.

As Jason told him about the upcoming windsurfing lesson, the calamari he'd tried for the first time, and the amazing sunset last night, Brian knew that his son was incapable of hurting Madeline.

He asked anyway. "I'm curious," he said. "Do you know Madeline Dominguez?"

Jason was silent. Then he said harshly, "Yeah, why?" He heard Rachel in the background asking Jason something. A muffled explanation and then Rachel taking the phone, her displeased voice: "Why are you asking about Madeline Dominguez?"

He lied, explaining that his friend's daughter knew someone who knew her.

"Tell your friend to keep his daughter away," Rachel said.

He didn't say anything, knowing that if he waited she'd give him more information. She sighed and he imagined her putting her hand to her forehead. He knew she'd gone to another room for privacy. It felt strange and exciting to be talking to her while in her dining room without her knowing.

"Trust me: this girl's trouble," she said. When he didn't respond, she continued, "She's a mess."

Then she told him that an image had gone viral at the high school.

"It's her," Rachel said. "Near the urinals in the locker room. A blow job. She's barely fifteen."

He had a flash of Jason after football practice, pressing and angling Madeline's head, and her holding the backs of his thighs.

Rachel seemed to know what he was thinking, because she said, "It wasn't Jason."

"You've seen it?"

"Jesus, no. You can't tell who it is, but it's not Jason."

He didn't respond.

"Listen," she said, "this girl's been texting him. He blocked her. The last thing he wants is to talk about her."

The rest of the morning Brian spent on the Internet, trolling for clues about Madeline. He found a comment thread from two women whose daughters had gone to Madeline's middle school:

> I don't want my daughter to end up like M.
> Is it true? BJ?
> Yes. Football players. More than one. Side of her
>   face, had to be another person for that angle.
> She was on Stacy's soccer team.
> She was so sweet. What happened?

After eating a sandwich and some potato chips and watching a documentary on Netflix, Brian went outside again to look at the pond. He still wanted to drain it. He thought he heard something, and he walked to the edge of the yard. With a rush of adrenaline, he watched Madeline in cutoffs and a T-shirt and the same teen boy, a ring at his lip and another at his eyebrow, slipping in and out of the trees and bushes near the house. They were looking downward, watching their feet.

He came close to them and then shook a branch to get their attention.

She leaned in to tell the boy something and they watched him. They seemed ready to bolt, so Brian moved quickly, his body surging. He lunged and grabbed the boy's arm.

The boy winced, bending at his waist and crouching, his backpack sliding off. "Asshole," he muttered. Brian held tight and used his other hand to unzip the backpack, finding toilet paper rolls and spray paint canisters.

When he looked up, Madeline's eyes met his. They stared at each other for a long moment, and he let go of the boy's skinny arm.

"Go," Brian said. "I won't say anything."

Madeline shook her head in disgusted confusion.

The boy slipped and then steadied a hand to the ground, recovering his balance. He stood, his face pinched, and retrieved his backpack, and then he and Madeline moved down the hill.

An hour or so later Brian returned from the hardware store with a hydraulic pump. He slumped the hose in the pond water and moved the base with his foot, turning it on. The machine coughed and sighed and sighed again. A humming noise began, which turned into a steady *boom-boom-boom* like the beating of a drum.

The water swirled around the hose, sucked inside. It surged and spat out onto the hill, where it began to trickle, leaving a trail. The trail spread and frothed and divided into three smaller trails.

A gaping hole would be left, and there was satisfaction in imagining Rachel and Jason coming home to find it.

The machine groaned, boomed loudly, and went silent. He tugged on the hose and it spurt out two gasps of algae-flecked water. Something had stuck, and when he crouched to investigate, he released the hose from the base and an old sock wound in hairy grass came loose in a splash of smelly water.

He found his stick and poked it inside to make sure he'd gotten all of the obstruction. It seemed clear. But the pause in his efforts dispirited him.

He was balanced at his knees, deciding what to do next, when Madeline approached, leaves flecked in her hair and on her arm.

"I'm Jason's dad," he said, standing.

"I've seen his dad," she said, matter-of-fact. "They're in Hawaii."

He was used to this mistake, but it stung nonetheless. "That's his stepdad." He was unable to keep the irritation from his voice.

"They left you," she said, looking away as if she didn't want to know whether her words had hurt him.

They were silent for a long time. She moved around the yard, examining a hanging birdhouse, picking up a shriveled orange and chucking it, bending to smell the roses near the back door.

She was looking at the pond—almost half gone—when she asked, "Are you going to finish emptying it?"

He didn't answer.

She said, "Why? It's just a pond."

When he spoke, his voice sounded amplified and oddly authoritative: "What did Jason do?" He kept his gaze steady, and she looked back, steely-eyed.

"I hate him," she answered. The air between them turned heavy with her indignation.

"Tell me what happened," he said. "Then I can help. I can do something."

Her face softened into a frown and she said, "It doesn't matter."

"What did he do?"

She looked sorry for him. "Don't worry about it," she said.

He felt the poignancy of their common ground, his longing and loneliness akin to hers. Sidelined on the periphery, squatting in a vacated house, wishing the house and family were his. *Leave me the fuck alone psycho slut.* But he kept quiet and she seemed to appreciate this.

For some time she pretended to ignore him, her thumbs flying across her cell phone keypad, but he knew he had her attention.

She looked at him sideways, continuing to fiddle with her phone. Then she extended her hand with the phone, showing him an image of Jason, shirtless, giving the bird with the middle fingers of both hands, an intimacy in his expression—carefree, humorous, playful—one that Brian faintly recognized.

She swung her hand away, saying, "If you're a girl and they decide they don't respect you, don't like you, forget it."

"Are you talking about Jason?" he asked.

She shrugged, noncommittal.

He sat beside the pond and poked his stick in the muck. Eventually she slid her phone in her back pocket and then sat cross-legged near him, plucking up the grass and creating a pile.

She looked at him, her head tilting as if she was trying to see him more clearly or observing something that didn't belong. His chest clenched as she scooted closer. What was she doing? With a peculiar combination of excitement and revulsion, he heard himself say, "Stop, no," almost at the same time she said, "There's dirt on you," her eyes narrowing, and then she rubbed with her fingers at his forehead.

When her hand left him, he asked, "Is it gone?"

Nodding, she shifted back to her original position, careful not to disturb her grass pile. She hesitated, then scooped and threw her pile at once, so that the blades speckled the surface of the pond.

The wind stirred the grass in random patterns, and he used his stick to fling the hairy sock. It made a plunking noise and sank. "Good luck," he said to the vanished sock, and she laughed.

"Have fun," she added.

She stayed longer than he expected, observing in silence while he gathered the pump and carried it to the garage. Later still, before she sidestepped the muddy pump-water trails and disappeared down the hill, she helped him uncoil the garden hose and watched while he refilled the pond.

Johnny Hitman

No matter where I'm living, Vivian's Christmas cards find me. It's always the same: a photograph of Vivian, her husband, their two kids—girl, boy—and their golden retriever. A biblical quote in advertisement of her faith (born-again Christian since the late nineties) is imprinted on the cards, and a personal handwritten message in gold or silver glitter ink; the latest, which I received yesterday addressed to New Beginnings, has a photograph of Vivian and her family on vacation in ski gear, kids around eight and nine, wide-eyed with wide smiles: *Dear Linda, I'm thinking* *of you and praying for your recovery! Remember, it's darkest before the dawn! Love Always, Viv.*

Qualities I dislike in others—self-righteousness, religiosity, conformity—I don't mind in Vivian; and she in turn has accepted me, which is no small feat considering the friends and family I've already lost. I'm an only child, and my parents, who are very wealthy, pay for my treatment; but despite the pleadings of my counselors, they refuse to have contact with me, which is why I refer to Family Day as Lonesome Day. In case I bear any illusions, I also just recently learned that they've issued a restraining order against me. At New Beginnings, we repeatedly watch *Clean and Sober* starring Michael Keaton on a donated television in the group meeting room during free time, and the veteran women recite the dialogue like they're at the *Rocky Horror Picture Show*. This is my fourth stay, court-mandated, thirty-three years old, no kids or significant other, thank God, injected heroin my drug of choice, alcohol and barbiturates a close second. I promised myself not to become one of the memorizers. But last night, Vivian's Christmas card in hand, I found myself absentmindedly mouthing along while watching Detox, the resident cat, behind the TV as he studied the outside from a windowsill, hind legs half lifted and raised fur on his shoulders and tail as if he'd spotted something dangerous.

Every two years or so (any day now), Vivian calls and we talk by phone. Her voice sounds animated, but I hear hollowness underneath, and when she falters I know she's ready to say goodbye. Her husband, a goofy-looking proctologist, is one of those insufferably proud UCLA graduates, and although I can never remember their kids' names until I read the cards (Brandon and

Isabella), I always remember that their dog's name is Bruin. Vivian supported her husband through medical school, working at tedious office-management jobs at the hospitals where he was in residence, but now she claims to be a happy stay-at-home mom, her plan all along.

As girls we made up games such as Invisible Cow, where by crossing a dry, brown patch of dead grass in her backyard, we became unseen and bovine, and had to cross back to regain our human status. She once shaved her entire body with her mother's rusting pink Gillette razor. She would lie down in an old decaying meat freezer in her garage, calling it her coffin. She said she used to like going to my house (though we spent most of our time in the chaos and freedom of hers) because it was quiet and we had better food. "All I remember about your parents," she said, "was how your dad was almost never home and he was this intellectual money wizard who was supposed to be better than everyone else, and your mom looked so pretty, but she hated when we bothered her and when our dirty fingerprints smudged the glass surface of her dining room table." Sometimes she felt sorry for me. Although her parents were loud drunks who caused her embarrassment, they weren't indifferent. "Rich people like your parents," she told me, "want the ego gratification of children without expending personal effort." We watched horror movies at her house, and she made up a series of vivid and terrifying stories about Johnny Hitman, a murderous rapist who roamed our streets. It was only later that I recognized his creation as a caution. "Girls are precious things," she used to say in her own type of movie tagline. "Sugar and spice and everything nice. Johnny Hitman has sex with them and then kills them."

Her careful construction of identity as an adult bears little resemblance to the girl I knew. When we speak by phone, she's guarded. Only once, about four years ago, triggered by the drug-overdose death of her older half brother, Rusty, did Vivian confide in me. She told me about a short-lived affair she'd had; about a general dissatisfaction; about her anguish regarding Rusty's estrangement; about her own regret over the past, and specifically for what had happened to me "that night with Rusty." Nothing happened, I reminded her. But she doesn't believe me. I certainly don't blame Rusty for my failures, or anyone else for that matter, and much worse things have happened to me, for the most part self-induced. Yet there's no denying that our lives changed that night.

We were twelve years old. Sadness had already been building inside me. I could have anticipated my future, but being here—the force of its arrival and the reality—is something entirely different. I didn't consider Vivian's future, but looking back, I could've predicted the careful exactitude, and the ways that she would lose as well.

DURING LUNCH RECESS we saw Rusty watching us behind the chain-link fence on the outskirts of the playground. Rusty, seventeen at the time, had been sent away, I didn't know where, but I assumed juvenile hall, for something really bad, but I wasn't sure what. He'd been gone for over a year. No one spoke of him, as if he'd never existed.

It was one of those hot, smoggy afternoons with the blacktop shuddering, and even from a distance I could see that Rusty wore his faded T-shirt with AC/DC on the front, the red letters separated by a gold lightning bolt. I thought I was in love with him, even though (or especially since) I knew I shouldn't be. His long and mysterious absence had increased my infatuation. Vivian resented it—the one true wedge in our friendship—and this, I decided, was why she'd not told me he was back.

Vivian wore a white sweater over her dress with the first two buttons buttoned, cape-like, her arms not in the sleeves. It looked like something an old woman would do. She picked up a red rubber ball and threw it at the fence—at him—and yelled at him to go away. I felt a surge of anger and called her a bitch. We didn't fight often, so when we did our fights quickly became physical, but they died just as fast. She grabbed me and scraped her fingernails down the skin of my forearm, hissing, "You don't know him," and I hissed back, "He's my friend." I loosened from her grip and ran to him.

He wore his father's baseball hat. Mr. Flaherty owned a forklift business (the hats had a yellow forklift on the front bill), and I felt sure that he wore it in mockery of his father. I slowed, feeling Vivian's eyes on my back, the scratch on my arm stinging, and I walked the last few steps, my heartbeat thrumming in my ears. His fingers slid through the diamonds of the chain link as he leaned into it. "Rich girl," he said. This was how he used to greet me, and I realized how much I'd missed him. He was the only one who openly recognized my parents' wealth. I smiled so hard my face hurt. I noticed a scar shaped like a boomerang near the corner of his eye that hadn't been there before. The recess monitor had spotted Rusty, and she blew her whistle and motioned for him to move on. He did, but I wasn't upset, knowing that I would go over to the Flahertys' after school and see him again. But later in math class, Vivian told me that Rusty was no longer welcome at home, so I could just forget about that.

AFTER SCHOOL VIVIAN and I walked to her house. When we went inside, she told me to wait in the hallway while she gave her parents the mail. Her parents' bedroom door was cracked and I could see the flickering bluish light from the television and the bumps of their feet beneath the covers of the bed. Their house was always dirty and smelled of nicotine. It was Friday, and I often spent the night, even though our parents had never met. When Mr. and Mrs. Flaherty asked me questions about my home life, no matter how vague and generic my responses, they seemed gratified, as if I'd proved them right. I was accustomed to hostility and gossip about my parents, and while it used to bother me, I understand that it was curiosity mixed with envy. Vivian quietly shut the bedroom door behind her and made a face, letting me know that her parents were hungover.

When Mrs. Flaherty was hungover, she was sullen and volatile: she'd slapped Vivian in front of me many times; but when drunk, she was fun, turning the stereo up and dancing with me. Once I remember her pretending to smoke a tampon like a cigar. She had permanently arched feet like a Barbie's from only wearing high heels, so it looked like she tiptoed. Mr. Flaherty wasn't fun drunk or hungover—an aura of shame. A large, lumbering man with unruly gray hair, he and Vivian were close. The camaraderie Mrs. Flaherty and I shared was compensation for our jealousy. I'd become such a fixture in their home that I was part of their dysfunction, and I somehow knew that Rusty wasn't Mr. Flaherty's biological son, though no one ever told me this information.

Vivian's grandmother Mayma was a ghost of a woman who slept in the guest bedroom. I don't remember ever seeing her leave the bed. Once in a while, Mayma would howl. Vivian would leave whatever we were doing and go inside her room to comfort her. It only took a few minutes. We loved to watch Mayma sleeping, her torso rigid above the tucked-in sheets and comforter, her mouth a dark pink *O*, and her hands crossed at her chest. Her quilted nightgown had frill at the wrists. Her breathing sounded hoarse—*hee, hoo, hee, hoo*—and if we waited and watched, she would suck in air, keeping it inside for the longest time, motionless. I'd worry that maybe this time she'd died, but whenever I looked at Vivian, she'd be smiling, and then Mayma's breath would finally come out in a long, gurgling *whoosh*.

We spent a lot of time in the Flahertys' garage. The Flahertys kept their trucks parked outside along the curb, and their small motorboat, *Living Large*, in the driveway on an orange metal carrier with wheels. That afternoon, we found Rusty playing pool in the garage, and he asked Vivian if she was going to be a baby and tell on him. She said that she wouldn't if he left right now. He ignored her, leaning over the pool table, the cue loose in his hands, and then he hit the ball quick and hard, the cue swinging up. It seemed so sad to me that he wasn't allowed home, and that he might get caught just to prove the point. I wanted Vivian to be kind to him, because that seemed to be what he wanted.

Vivian looked upset—her head hung down—and I thought she might cry. She almost never cried. Rusty noticed as well because he set his cue on the table and walked over to her. He promised to leave after he finished his game. I saw the way he let his fingers touch her cheek underneath her hair. She didn't raise her head, but she nodded. When she finally did look up, I saw that she hadn't cried. He left soon after.

Later that night, Vivian and I set up blankets and pillows on the floor of the living room to watch *Friday the 13th*. Vivian had made a bowl of popcorn smothered with butter. The popcorn felt warm and wet and when I said so, she said not to worry, that was just the blood she put on it. She pushed play on the DVD player, and there was a close-up of something pink and large going in and out of a red, hairy thing. Slick and pulsating like a detailed view of a gigantic worm. She stopped the movie and took it out, exchanging it with ours. I'd not seen porn before and asked what it was. "A man's penis entering a woman's vagina," she said in a clinical voice. "It's *his* movie," she said in this way that made it seem like it was mine also, because I liked Rusty.

We watched the final scene in *Friday the 13th* over and over, stopping and rewinding: A woman floats in a canoe in the middle of a lake, soft music playing and the water lapping. Suddenly a figure comes out of the lake and a scabbed arm grabs the woman around her throat and drags her under the water. Each time, one of us made a noise or squirmed, so we kept testing ourselves. We were watching it for the sixth or seventh time, concentrating and trying not to flinch, when the sliding glass door slid open and Rusty emerged from behind the curtain.

I screamed and for a long second I saw black. Vivian also screamed so that her scream and mine blended. An angry voice came from the Flahertys' bedroom (I couldn't tell if it was her mom or dad) ordering us to shut up, and it calmed me. Vivian called back, "Sorry," but she didn't say that Rusty had frightened us. Her face looked like it had just been glued together. We were sitting cross-legged in front of the television, and she put a hand on my knee. "Leave," she told Rusty, her voice steely, "or I'm telling Dad." Our commotion triggered Mayma, who began to howl. I felt my heart beating in my ears, the same as when I'd met Rusty at the playground fence, when Vivian left to help Mayma, telling me that she'd be right back and to ignore Rusty.

Rusty went to the kitchen and I watched him go inside their walk-in pantry, keeping the door open. I didn't hesitate. When I entered, he shut the door, and I was scared, but I also felt something of the heady recklessness in my future. He reached for my arm, pulling me close. My back against him, his mouth near my ear, I heard him taking shallow breaths. One of his hands fiddled with the button and zipper on my jeans. I closed my eyes and thought about his movie and the pink throbbing worm. I wondered if I'd have to do that to get him to love me. "Hold still," he said, pushing me into a half bend, his hand digging inside me. I gasped in pain and then we heard tapping on the pantry door and Vivian whispering my name. His fingers left me and he set both his hands on the doorknob so that she couldn't open it.

"She doesn't want you," he said. "She wants me."

"Not true," she said, the doorknob rattling with her effort, and then I heard her feet on the kitchen tile and I worried that she would be mad at me for a very long time.

Soon after, the pantry door burst open and Mr. Flaherty pulled me out. He wore a green bathrobe with the sash undone and I could see his striped boxer shorts and his gray chest hairs.

I quickly righted my underwear and jeans. Vivian looked like she hadn't meant to tell on Rusty and she wished she could take it back.

Mr. Flaherty stooped to my height, his hands gripping me. The whites of his eyes had red streaky lines. He kept squeezing my arms and asking if I'd been hurt, and I kept shaking my head, saying, "Nothing happened, nothing happened." Rusty tried to walk away, but Mr. Flaherty let me go and grabbed his elbow. He smacked him across the face with the palm of his hand. Rusty hunched over, a purple mark where Mr. Flaherty's horseshoe-shaped ring had dug into his cheek. "Fuck you," he said, but it came out miserable. He stood, moved his hand to his cheek, and started for the side door. "Fuck you," he said again before leaving, but it came out quiet and just as miserable.

Mr. Flaherty had closed his robe and I was glad that I couldn't see his boxers and hairy chest. He cradled his head with his hands. Then his face lifted and he stared at Vivian for a long second, as if to say, Tell her. But he didn't want to be there when she did, so he left us. When I looked at Vivian, I saw that she was struggling to speak, and I wished that she didn't have to. When she said, "I'm only going to say this once, and you have to promise not to ever tell anyone," I understood that Rusty's attention to me had been an attempt to get to her, and that he was very dangerous. I could feel the way our friendship would change, a distance already beginning. But I didn't know that my parents would move to a different state in a few months anyhow: to a bigger home in an affluent neighborhood where we weren't the wealthiest family, only one of many. I thought about the quiet nothing of my home, the loneliness I felt. I wanted to live with the Flahertys and listen to Mayma's strange breathing. I wanted to take a knife to Johnny Hitman's throat and tell him, You don't scare me.

AT NEW BEGINNINGS, I share a room with a junkie, older and angrier and smarter than me, and she said, "Why'd you put that card on our dresser?" She's been pining for an argument: along with other reasons, she resents how, unlike her, money has insulated me from jail time. "It's stupid," she said, "those people pretending to be happy and perfect. Fuck them. I know you hate that stuff." She thumped her finger at Vivian's face as if flicking off a booger. "Why's this bitch get a pass?" I reminded her that she has photos of her nieces and nephews on our shared dresser, and she said, "Too bad you don't. You got a restraining order from your folks, though. Why don't you frame that and put it next to your card?"

When Vivian calls, the generic nature of our conversation will belie our inability to shake the intimacy of our girlhood friendship. I choose to believe that Rusty purposely got caught that night, and that by permanently cutting his ties with his family, he protected Vivian, because he wouldn't be around to damage her more. But Vivian and I won't talk about this. "I'll pray for you," she'll probably tell me, and I'll say, "Sure, go ahead," because with anyone else, I'd probably say fuck off, but with Vivian, I don't mind. I'll remember how we ran to the kitchen window when we heard the roar of Rusty's motorcycle. The half moon looked dirty, trapped in some branches from a tree. He took off with a jump, and when he turned the corner, he went so close to the ground it looked like his shoulder touched the road.

TREES

I was a busboy when I was fourteen, working after my school day ended, sometimes until late into the night. My manager, Francisco, Salvadorian and stocky, wore a cross necklace, visible at the end of his shift when he removed his tie and unbuttoned his dress shirt. I tried my best for him. I often substituted father figures for my absent one. Francisco hired me on the spot. He paid me under the table.

We worked in the background while the pretty women served the food and drink in the front, aspiring actresses and models, mostly white and young, working temporarily until a marriage proposal or some other significant life-changing event. An undercurrent of power and lust vibrated between them and the Latino busboys and kitchen staff, including me. I hated and desired them, and I looked forward to their commands, and to our bodies rubbing against each other when we passed in the tightly spaced kitchen. They mingled with the wealthy clientele, swaying from table to table, chatting up the customers, gossiping about each other. A soft competition going on at all times.

One night I catered a celebrity function with Francisco in the gigantic backyard of a Beverly Hills mansion. I'd been warned by the others to be careful of our employer, Julie Campos. She had a reputation for being a real bitch. She told me to take my tray and stand in between these palm trees at the edge of the yard and wait for her signal. Her lipstick matched the maroon of the dress she wore. She had four rings on the fingers of her left hand and two on her right. She called me "darling." But what do you want me to do? I asked. Darling, she said, a hand at my shoulder, your job is to disappear.

A long time went by, more than an hour. Behind me, I knew, was a spectacular view of downtown Los Angeles, lights shimmering. But I didn't turn and look. There was a rose bush and three more trees and, in between, a section of tables and people. I couldn't really see the celebrities because their backs were to me. The tables had been spread with food, bottles of wine and champagne, and wineglasses and glass flutes. Slender white candles glimmered everywhere. I heard flickers of conversations. A man with a British accent talked about his vision for his screenplay. A woman said she believed lesbians had lived so many past lives as men that they were not yet comfortable in their newly acquired female bodies. Julie Campos went from table to table, handling the people, whispering in their ears, laughing. The wind picked up, swaying the lights hanging from the trees. I searched for Francisco but couldn't find him.

I might've left had it not been for Francisco. I wanted so badly to please him. After more time, I began to feel as if I were a part of the property. An odd feeling, as if I were no more than a palm tree or a vase or carpet or wallpaper. Money had purchased me. The clinking of silverware and glassware and the constant hum of voices accentuated the impression. I'm a tree, I thought. Here I am. Don't move. A tree.

I saw my father sitting in his chair in our living room the year before he left us, staring into the distance. He was a landscape gardener, and as a kid I would go with him to job sites, waiting in his truck and reading books. One afternoon four days before my eighth birthday, we were driving on the outside lane of the 110 freeway, when a man stepped in front of my father's truck with his arms raised. My father swerved, but we hit him. A loud thump, I can hear it now. His body rolled up our windshield. I screamed. My father braked and swerved again. The man's body rolled down. My father put his truck in reverse and backed up, parking on the shoulder of the road behind the man. I got out of the truck and followed my father to a puddle of black with the man curled into himself. His chest moved. His leg twitched. Then he went still. It smelled like alcohol and copper from his blood. My father told me to go sit in the truck. I watched out the cracked windshield as the police and ambulances arrived. My father looked like he might cry, but he didn't.

A paramedic tapped on my window. I rolled it down and he asked me my name, so I told him. Do you need anything? he asked. Are you okay? I told him no, and that I was fine. It wasn't your dad's fault, he said. He stared at me for a minute, and then he left. I kept the window cracked. The sky had gone dusky gold and the air had a chill to it. I prayed for the man and watched as they put him on a stretcher and then carried his body off the street.

In my prayer I talked not to God but to the man: I told him that I wanted him to be safe, that I knew he'd made a mistake by walking in front of our truck, and that I hoped he'd get better. But I knew he would not get well and that he'd wanted to die. He might've been dead already. But I never asked.

Back at home, my heart pounded as I listened from my bedroom wall vent to my parents in the kitchen. They had no idea I could hear them. Usually we spoke English in our house, but that night they spoke in Spanish. I learned the man's age, thirty-nine, and his name, Justin McCord, and that he'd most likely died from a skull fracture. There'd been a suicide note in his pocket. His wife had left him the month before.

Un borracho empedernido, my father said sadly, *como yo.* A long silence and then my mother began to cry. *No es lo mismo,* she said.

A chill went through me, spreading into my arms and legs. My father disappeared sometimes for days, but I'd not known why, nor had I seen him drunk. A periodic alcoholic, he did that away from us. I realized that I didn't know him at all. The coldness moved to my feet. I had the desire to run into the kitchen and punch his face. I must have known then that he would leave.

Not more than three weeks later, he was gone. He sent money in the mail, no return address. My mother did okay without him.

We did okay. But for months after he left, I woke in the mornings and felt his desertion anew. I longed for him. No matter how I tried, I couldn't shake my love for him.

I continued to pray to the man who'd stepped in front of our truck and died, Justin McCord. He became Uncle Justin, and I'd tell myself stories about him. Uncle Justin had once lived in Thailand. He liked Chinese food and video games and the Dodgers. As a kid he'd fallen from a tree and chipped his front tooth. Even now—all these years later—Uncle Justin is real to me.

But it was that night at the party that Uncle Justin spoke to me.

I stood and became a tree. It felt like years passed. At one point Julie Campos looked directly at me and held my gaze. I felt my face go red. No signal and then she left.

So I prayed to Uncle Justin, asking for something to happen. In the dark, he whispered back. He said he was sorry and that he loved me. Then he told me that I should stop praying to him. He was behind me, talking into my ear.

Why? I asked, surprised to feel a tear roll down my face. I'm not real, he said. Then why are you talking to me? Why can I hear you? He sighed. I'm glad, he said, that you ask. You're dreaming. Hallucinating. I shook my head. No, I said. I'm awake. I felt stupid, as though I'd failed him or misunderstood our relationship. Your father's not coming back, he said. I know, I said. He sighed again. Well, he said, I should be going. Okay, I said, bye, because I wanted him gone. I felt the weight of his hand on my shoulder, and then the grizzled brush of his stubble against my cheek. I blinked the tears away, turning to face him, but he'd left. That was the last time I prayed to him.

Eventually Francisco found me. He raised his voice, angry:

You've been standing here this whole time? he asked. I explained about Julie Campos. In the dark, I could see the glint of his cross on its chain. He looked tired, his eyes bulged, and he smelled like booze. I almost told him about Uncle Justin. I longed to let my tears come like a little boy, and to have him comfort me. He must've seen it in my face, because he put his heavy hands on my shoulders. Never, ever, he said, will I understand rich people. He drove me home, his Oldsmobile Cutlass rattling in the black of the night, a Vin Scully bobblehead dancing on his dashboard.

A few days later, my mother and I found out that my father had died in a bar fight, stabbed in the arms and chest. The officer who accompanied my father to the hospital was fond of him and he came to our home to tell us. Your dad was good-natured and kind, the officer said, standing in our doorway. It was an overcast day, spitting a little rain, so my mother invited him inside, but he declined. How did you know him? I asked. He spent a lot of time in the back of my patrol car, the officer admitted.

Most of the time I used photographs to remember my father. But now he came to me as clearly as the officer standing before me. He looked at me and smiled sadly and then like a flash, he left. I felt my body sway, so I steadied myself against the door-frame. When did it happen? I asked, but I already knew. When Uncle Justin tried to warn and protect me.

HALF-TRUTH

When Kelly checks, Owen, her six-year-old son, is in his bed reading, his leg extended from his comforter. He sets his book down, spread open to keep his place. She sees the seriousness of his face, and because his bangs are combed back—damp from his shower and ridged from the comb—he seems vulnerable and adultlike.

Owen has stopped sleeping in her bed, but they've broken the rule because he had the flu. He vomited three times—twice in the toilet, once on the floor—and although one full day and night has passed vomit-free, she knows he dreads the possibility.

This is his first night back in his bed.

She watches the slight lift and fall of his chest.

"You were brave," she says.

He stares at her.

"I know how much you hate to throw up," she explains.

"Mom," he says in an impatient and world-weary tone, continuing to stare with what now looks like pity—maybe compassion; after a pause he adds, "I didn't have a choice."

His answer surprises her. She hates how he refuses to let her be the parent. Why can't he fake being a child, same as how she fakes being an adult? Now that she's in her twenties, Kelly better understands the consequences of being a teenage mom, knowing that this defines and shapes her life more than anything else. She tries to hide the emotion on her face, remembering how Owen begged her to stay in the bathroom with him every time he felt nauseated, and how he cried and panicked and cursed, making his voice a grim mockery of hers: *Goddamn, goddamn, goddamn.*

Owen's hand goes to his stomach.

"You can't get the stomach flu twice," she says. When this doesn't help, she adds, "You're not going to throw up again."

"How do you know?" He shakes his head. "How can you be sure?"

She wishes he hadn't lost Blue Bear. No one can remember where the stuffed animal came from, so she can't replace it. Blue Bear used to make him feel better.

She leans over, and as she's about to kiss his lips he turns his face so that she lands at his ear.

•

EVEN THOUGH IN retrospect Kelly got pregnant in an attempt to hold on to Nick, maybe to save him, by the time she was four months along, she wanted the baby to be a girl: to cut all connections and reminders, including the commonality of male sex. Yet Owen looks like Nick, even more so the older he gets: full bottom lip, hazel eyes, features that attracted her in the first place.

Kelly never injected heroin, only snorted it to accompany Nick, and then sobered up, pregnant at seventeen. She finished high school with a swollen belly, while he dropped out and moved from his home to the streets.

He's not allowed visitations until he tests clean.

After Owen was born, she was relieved to discover that she loved her son—a straightforward love, different from how she felt about Nick: that other kind of love made her crazy and irrational. It took from her life. What she feels for Owen is bound with guilt and responsibility. It provokes a desire to protect and nourish, deep and real, and it comes from her.

At around three years old, Owen started asking, "Mommy, do I have a daddy? Where's my daddy?"

She sidetracked with vague and broad responses.

But in the last year, he asked more questions.

After consulting with her parents, she decided to be as honest as possible, explaining that Nick was a sick man, addicted to drugs—by this time Owen knew in a general way about drugs—and that she was sorry.

Owen pointed out various men on the streets: "Is that him? That my dad?" Sometimes he'd shout, "There he is! There's Dad!" Her heart would thump and then she'd see a businessman crossing the street or a construction worker wiping his forehead.

So she found an old photograph of Nick that she'd taken for her photography class—Nick walking toward her, his hand held out. Right after she'd taken it, Nick had said, "Stop," and taken the camera from her.

Owen, sitting on the couch when she handed him the photo, held it in both hands close to his face. After a fixed pause, his only comment: "Dads should not have long hair. All the dads—Jim's dad and Henry's dad, all the dads—they don't have long hair."

He set the photo in his lap and gave her a look: repugnance, anger, grief. An acknowledgment—right in his eyes—that he felt sad and responsible for her.

A month or so later, as if he'd been thinking about it all that time, Owen asked Kelly if she used drugs, and she said a long time ago, but that she didn't anymore.

The questions dwindled.

Then three days ago, Owen asked, "Do you still see my daddy?" and she said, "No, no way. I don't want to see him," a lie.

Not only did she see Nick, but she thought about him constantly. Showing Owen that picture had sparked feelings she thought she was done with, as if they'd been waiting for her to catch her breath from Owen's infanthood.

Owen didn't ask more questions, but the guilt pressed like a weight. God, the way he looked at her! What made it worse: she was certain Owen knew she'd lied, same as how she knew when he took more chocolate chips after she told him no more.

About a month ago, Nick must have found out that she'd been calling his friends to ask about him, because he came into Vons and waited in her line. When it was his turn, he didn't have anything for her to scan, and she watched him walk out, pausing at the door to flash one of his rare smiles at Toby, the mentally challenged grocery bagger.

The next thing she knew, she was in the alleyway behind the produce trucks and the garbage bins where no one could see them, showing Nick photos of Owen on her iPhone. He admitted that he'd watched Owen at school recess from across the street, until the recess monitor noticed him. When she saw that he was crying, tears slid down her own face. He put his hand under her shirt and she didn't stop him. As it was happening, she knew she could never tell anyone. He was high, although he did his best to hide it. She let her fingers touch him. He put his weight on her, his face pressed into her neck; then she took him inside her—she wished she could forget this part—so that she could carry him away with her, even when she knew she was supposed to hate him. She was more than an hour late back to work, and she agreed to work a double for the cashier who covered for her.

Kelly imagined her parents saying: "You're risking every-thing, all your hard work, for a nobody, a nothing. Hasn't he done enough to ruin your life?" They helped pay for her apartment. She took night classes twice a week at the community college. Her friends set her up on blind dates with young lawyers and tax accountants. She sensed the men judging whether she was pretty enough for their efforts and didn't return their calls. She'd only had sex with Nick, couldn't imagine being with another man or desiring another man; and while normally this might be con-sidered discretionary and modest, she knew that her family and friends were waiting for Nick to die from an overdose, or in some other violent manner, confirming their good sense. She didn't blame them. Her mom made her attend a church singles group:

men and women in their twenties and thirties, already scarred and bitter from divorces, covering with vague smiles and talk of Jesus.

KELLY CAN'T SLEEP; and then, unsurprisingly, Owen opens her bedroom door. Even in the darkness she sees he's naked— most likely discarding his pajamas during a bathroom visit; she imagines them crumpled on the floor—and that his expression is worried.

Kelly scoots over to give him room. It strikes her as near impossible that his penis—as innocuous as his fingers and toes— will become a man's penis.

He makes a wheezy noise, forcibly breathing through his nose. "Can't sleep," he says, taking his place in her bed. The distinctiveness of his voice reminds her of how she can spot him instantly in a crowd—a flash of knowing—before distinguishing the tip of his head or a swing of his arm.

Their faces are close and his eyes assess her. "You okay?" he asks, and he seems like an old man peering at her. "You okay?" He speaks sincerely, his breath a little bad, though it also smells of toothpaste. "I can tell when something's bothering you," he says. He smiles, an extravagantly bizarre little smile, and then adjusts his head on her pillow.

She turns from him, stirrings of resentment. "You're not supposed to worry about me," she says, talking to the ceiling. "Remember," she says, "you're the kid. I'm the parent."

He snorts: part laugh, part acknowledgment.

She turns back to face him.

He props himself on his elbow. "Mom, is Taco in heaven?"

Taco, her parents' Chihuahua-beagle, was buried two years earlier in her parents' backyard after a cancerous tumor distended his stomach and killed him. Owen asks questions about Taco's death to elicit the same comforting, unvarying response, as if they'd agreed on one consistent, security-inducing platitude.

"Taco is in our hearts," she says, thinking of all the lies and half-truths that people tell kids to make life and death palatable. Santa Claus and the Easter Bunny and the Tooth Fairy—preparations for bigger lies. That's why she wanted to be honest about Owen's father, though now she wonders if she should have lied.

"Nothing really dies," he says, finishing for her, "because it lives on in our hearts forever."

KELLY STARTLES AWAKE before the alarm goes off, her skin wet with sweat. Owen's body presses against hers, his fingers tangled in her hair, his arm flung across her chest, a leg pressed against her thigh. She wants away, wants out, and then a sickening and familiar realization: Owen will be with her. Every day. No matter what.

THAT MORNING AT work Nick comes in, and when it's his turn in Kelly's line, he stands there, high—his eyes black dots. Do you have money? he mouths, so that the people behind him won't hear. When he walks away, a sweat breaks at the back of her neck.

She goes on her break and he's waiting, leaned up against the wall with a leg bent, foot on the brick, his pants sliding down his hips—skinny, pathetic. But she has a twenty-dollar bill in her sweater pocket and she lets her fingers touch it as she walks to him.

The black vinyl seats of her old Cadillac are cracked from the sun, a yellowish cushion showing through. The air conditioner barely works; she turns the key in her ignition and there's a whooshing noise. She's already given him the twenty, and he's leaned forward, fiddling with her radio. He keeps fiddling, not looking at her. He radiates an energy that drives everything and everyone else from her mind.

"It doesn't work," she says.

He leans over and picks up an old dented juice box, then opens the car door and leaves, taking the juice box with him— she watches him throw it in a garbage bin as he walks from the parking lot.

She remembers being so lonely as a child and in adolescence, and for no good reason—her parents loved her, she had friends. Then she met Nick. Sometimes when he'd kiss her, she'd feel like her chest would crack open. Their intimacy and passion crushed her loneliness, giving her purpose and direction and a sense of reckless elation.

She opens her car door, a gust of wind passing, and she has to close her eyes because of the sun glinting off the other cars.

ALL THAT WEEK Nick and Kelly sit in her Cadillac on her lunch breaks and talk, mainly about Owen. She gives him money— fives and tens—without him asking. She pretends not to care, and when he offers her a sip from a miniature bottle of vodka, the kind they give on airplanes, he seems confused when she says no. "It's not like you're using drugs," he says. "I'm not corrupting you."

Instead she smokes Marlboro Reds, one after the other, the smoke lifting out her cracked window.

They kiss, nothing more—long sweeping kisses, so that when she thinks about him later, it seems like she's hallucinated this part.

She's used to talking about Owen, especially with her parents, but it's more gratifying with Nick, like she stored the information and now the one person who really appreciates is listening.

She talks about Owen's dive-bomb hugs when she picks him up from school; and how just yesterday, from her rearview mirror she watched him in the backseat staring out his window; and he seemed so far away, so lost in thought, that she asked him what he was thinking. But he didn't hear her, continuing to stare.

She tells him how before sleeping, Owen waves his right hand and fingers through the air, watching with half-closed eyes, as if making shapes or casting spells.

She tries to be honest, she says, but Owen keeps asking about Taco.

"Your parents' dead dog?"

She nods.

"What do you tell him?"

She says that they have, over time, developed a story that they tell each other (she can't remember who made it up), about death not being death. How they decided nothing really dies.

Nick surprises her, saying, "That's not lying."

"It's not the truth."

"There's a bigger honesty," he says, "in making a person feel better."

THAT SAME WEEK each time Kelly drives Owen home from school, he makes faces—nose scrunched—for her to see in her rearview mirror, letting her know that he smells the cigarettes.

But she's getting better at lying and hiding everything from her face. Besides, hers are little secrets; it's not like she's using drugs.

On Friday Owen tells her something that makes her heart race. He got sent to the principal's because three bullies—third graders—surrounded him and threw handballs at him. He punched the ringleader in the neck.

For a second, Owen says, the kid couldn't breathe, hands at his throat. Then the kid ran to the office and told on him.

Owen's conversation with the principal went like this:

"Why'd you hit him in the neck?"

"My mom told me I should stand up for myself. He hit me, so I hit back."

"She's wrong. Very wrong."

KELLY CASHIERS ON Saturday and Owen stays with her parents. On her break she and Nick sit in her Cadillac and she tells him about the bullies. Nick says that she has to confront the principal.

"You do it," she says.

"Right," he says.

"Then don't tell me what to do."

She doesn't want to listen to anything Nick says after that. She knows he's wearing a jacket to hide the marks on his arms.

"Forget it," she says, and she hangs her head.

When she looks up, he's fumbling with his jacket pocket. Out comes a stuffed purple bear with a tag attached to its ear. He passes it to her and she gets a flash of his grimy fingernails.

"Tell Owen," he says, "some story. Tell him it's Blue Bear, but that he turned purple."

She doesn't remember telling Nick about Blue Bear, and she imagines he stole the substitute from Toys "R" Us.

Owen, she knows, will never fall for it.

ON MONDAY KELLY finds the principal standing near the flagpole, watching parents and kids, occasionally waving and calling out hello. As she walks to him, he acknowledges her with a smile. He wears a suit and tie, and his chin and cheeks have a flushed, raw-skin look, probably from a recent shave. It's cold and there's a foggy morning drizzle. Some of the parents use umbrellas.

"Owen told me what happened," she says.

"Sorry?"

"How he punched a kid and got sent to your office."

He squints. The drizzle looks silver. A few children shout until someone blows a whistle.

She tells him what Owen told her, including how the bullies are third graders.

"Didn't happen." He sounds almost apologetic.

Before she leaves she has Owen come out of his classroom and she speaks with him by the drinking fountain, underneath the extended roof so that they won't get wet. She wants to know if there are real bullies. Within a few seconds, simply by looking at him, she understands he lied.

"Am I in trouble?" he asks. His breath comes out in little pockets of white and he stares at her with solemnity.

Before he goes back inside, she ties his shoe.

As she drives to work she wonders if she should punish Owen, but then she thinks about her own lies, and what Nick said about some lies being more like the truth.

With a pang of excitement, she wonders if Nick has been meeting with Owen without the recess guard noticing. That would be how he knew about Blue Bear. But it doesn't seem likely.

Then she thinks crazily of bringing Nick home. But she knows he'll be high, his clothes hanging off him, his shoes held together with duct tape.

She misses Nick—longs for the person he used to be. She craves that exhilarating sense of being in love. But he's someone else now, an echo of his old self, and she's someone else, too.

She needs to stop seeing him. She remembers him saying, "I was born bad, I live bad, and I'll die bad," and how, when she was a freshman in high school, this excited her; but now that she's the mother of his child, it's just stupid.

Nick taught her that her heart is resilient; but if she isn't careful, he'll incrementally wear it down.

After school she gives Owen the stuffed bear, and he sets it atop his stack of toys, indifferent, not asking where she got it. But later she watches him swinging the stuffed animal through the air as if making it fly; and that night she checks on Owen in his room and finds him sleeping, the purple bear at the foot of his bed.

CONFETTI

I'm going to tell you about when I went to talk to Father Bill at his office in a building in downtown Los Angeles. It wasn't about confession. Father Bill's a recovering alcoholic and he meets with people who need help. He'd been bad off a long time ago, passing out in his soup at Catholic functions, and once nearly burning down his parish. But then he sobered up. It doesn't matter if you're Catholic or atheist or whatever, he'll try to help. I met him outside a poetry reading, only three of us in the audience. A dark night, the moon flashing between clouds like a glimpse of a woman's hoop earring. Father Bill smoked a cigarette and watched me.

We stood beneath a street light in its dirty-yellow glow. "What's your name?" he asked. "Gabriel," I said, and we got to talking. He wore his priest collar, but he had on a short-sleeved shirt, a nicotine patch visible on his bicep. Balding like me (though he has more hair), midseventies, with brown, sorrowful eyes, and what looked like a cataract clouding the left one. Bad teeth: small, yellow, overlapping. He talked in a low, quiet voice, so I had to lean forward to hear him. He said when you quit some vice, like when he quit smoking, or when you lose something, experience a big loss, it's better not to try to find a replacement, such as chewing gum or jogging or whatever. Then he took a drag from his cigarette, but he didn't say anything about how he was smoking again. He said you should feel the area surrounding you, a unique experience, a feeling that won't happen again. He called the space "an expansiveness." He said you're in a position to feel God. He asked me, "Are you willing, Gabriel, to feel any kind of emotion?" "I don't know," I said, and then he said that I could come talk to him at his office.

So I did, calling and scheduling an appointment late on a Thursday morning, because I had a lot on my mind. The diocese offices are in the same building as a RadioShack and a Big 5 Sporting Goods store. I got lost in the hallway. A squat man wearing a priest collar saw me, and I said, "I don't know where I am. I'm looking for Father Bill." "No one really knows," he said, "where he's going." A pause for consideration, and then he directed me to the elevators and let me know what to do—"Go to level M, then turn left"—and then, to my surprise and embarrassment, he hugged me awkwardly and said, "Peace be with you," so I said, "Peace be with you, also," and he said, "Thanks."

Father Bill and I sat in chairs facing each other, a map of Los Angeles behind his desk. "What's going on?" he asked. So I told him how I'm a writer and a professor in the creative writing department of a private college not far from his office. I told him about Rebecca, another writer, who changed her name to Zaqar, because she said she was no longer Rebecca, this woman, now she was Zaqar. We'd gotten together when she was still Rebecca. Maybe I'd fallen for her—it was a long time ago. She'd been a visiting lecturer, one book under her belt, an awful memoir called *Small Dreams* about peeing on men and other bad relationship dramas, and everyone—readers, writers—judged her, probably laughed at her, too. Didn't she know she was profiting off her humiliation? She wasn't a bad writer—she and I shared our work—but her writing got more whacked-out, so that I couldn't follow, reminding me of someone shooting a confetti gun into the air. She drank and drugged during classes, and she'd allegedly gotten fired for selling LSD to her students and fucking them—couldn't get a job anywhere else after that.

I thought he might be shocked or offended by my story, or my use of the F-word, but Father Bill just nodded, and then he got up to get us water bottles from a miniature refrigerator in the corner. He flipped the blinds closed on his way back. Then he sat and stared at the space between his feet. He appeared to be concentrating and he nodded for me to proceed.

I told him about how, not long ago, I'd gone to open up my office and found Zaqar lying facedown near my desk, her skirt hiked up. I hadn't seen her in over a year—the last time, we'd had a fight about her drinking and I'd broken up with her for good. A big woman, lots of flesh. Her brother was a football player, she'd told me once, for the Miami Dolphins, and she hated him, though she loved his dog, a Doberman pinscher named Wanda. I had a young student with me—a wannabe punk rocker with a half-shaved head and black eyeliner all around her eyes—who plugged her nose, because Zaqar smelled like booze, rotten eggs, bananas, and shit. "You should go," I told my student, while kneeling to pull Zaqar's skirt down. But my student seemed determined and wouldn't leave. Her dad's a big-time lawyer—she'd written about him more than once—and I imagined her suing the school for distress or something, and when I looked at her, she seemed disgusted and impatient. She wanted to discuss her story, not deal with Zaqar—and she didn't recognize her: Zaqar'd been fired before she'd been a student. The next thing I know I'm nudging Zaqar with my foot, but she's not budging. I knelt next to her. She'd gained more weight, and her stomach was spread on the floor pancake-like. But it was probably her liver ballooning from her body. Her pink scalp shone beneath bristly hair, and her face was scratched and dirty. For some reason, I remembered her sitting in my Volvo after we'd had a fight and telling me how I settled for small dreams, like the title of her memoir. She quoted a passage from Henry James—she was well-read—something about a secret habit of sorrow, and the sharp pain of missing opportunities; losing so much and doing so much for so little, and it had me so angry then, and I got angry all over again. I stood and called security from the phone in my office.

Omar showed up, his uniform pants hanging, his red-tinged Afro grown out, skin a rich and dark color, his white Adidas spotless. He was holding a clipboard like he was going to take notes. "Ah, sweet Jesus," he said, setting his clipboard on my desk and then rolling Zaqar onto her back. The air filled with Zaqar's stinky, loud breathing. My student put her hand over her mouth and nose. I knew that Omar remembered Zaqar, and he stood and looked at her for an anguished minute. Omar's in his forties, only a little older than me, but he can treat me like a stupid teenager. He told my student to leave and that he'd take care of everything, and she finally did leave, but not before we rescheduled our appointment on her cell phone calendar.

Omar shook Zaqar, slapped her face, sprinkled some of my bottled water on her, and managed to wake her. Her mouth made an O and then went back to its crease. She sat up and stared at us, her eyes red. Her skirt looked like it had been singed, her shirt had dark purplish stains at the front, and her clear plastic sandals bit into her swollen ankles. She used to be the kind of woman who could look beautiful one minute, ugly the next, depending on lighting and angles, but now she just looked tragic.

"How'd you get in?" I asked. She put her head down and said, "Everything hurts." I wasn't sure if she was being sarcastic, so I said, "That's not what I asked." She said, "I just fuck up." "Tell that to the police," I said, thinking about how she'd used me, and then gone off with other men. Omar was looking at me with disgust, instead of her, so I said, "What? I'm not the one who trespassed." He didn't say anything but slowly helped Zaqar stand and guided her out of my office.

I followed them and said, "Call the police. She's a criminal"— and then again to Zaqar, "How'd you get in?" Omar had a hand on her back, and he turned to me and said, "You want me to put her in jail?" I nodded, and he just kept staring at me with hard eyes. "Why don't you talk to Bubby?" he said. Bubby, the oldest and most well-known writer on our staff, and my friend, had been the one to get Zaqar the lecturer position. Bubby was partial to Zaqar, and Omar was using it against me.

I followed them all the way to Omar's security cart. Omar helped position Zaqar in the front, and then he sat beside her and turned the key that he'd left in the ignition—a pile of clothes, a car battery, a For Sale sign, and empty crushed soda cans in a clear plastic bag in the back. Zaqar's face went to her hands. Omar released the brake and pressed the gas too hard, making the cart jerk from the curb. "She does it again," I called out, watching them turn the corner, "I'll call the cops."

AFTER I TOLD him this part, Father Bill leaned back in his chair and gave me a poker face. He finished off his water bottle, scratched at his nicotine patch, and nodded for me to continue. I told him how, the next afternoon, Bubby came to my office to talk to me. Omar had ratted on me. Bubby said that Zaqar was homeless, and that Omar had had to finally drop her off in an alleyway. All the detox places wouldn't take her, since she'd come and gone and come and gone, and I knew her family had been done with her years before. She had no more friends. Bubby said that I shouldn't be so heartless. "You're still licking your wounds," he said, "because she hurt your manly pride. So the fuck what. You desert her?" If she came back, he said, I shouldn't be such a dickwad. "What's wrong with you?" he asked. "You've got a place to sleep, a job, your health." Then he stole the pack of gum off my desk and left.

The next morning I had my fiction class, and we workshopped

a western thriller fantasy with cowboy vampires, and then a rip-off of Denis Johnson, a story about a heroin addict nicknamed Jesus John because of his bearded resemblance to Christ. Finished, I went to my Volvo in the parking lot, shaded beneath a tree, and saw Zaqar lying asleep inside—the passenger seat down, her mouth ajar. I didn't jump or anything, almost like I'd expected to find her. My sunroof is broken, but she'd managed to crack it open.

Omar happened to be patrolling the parking lot in his cart, and I waved him over. He stood and walked to me, and when he saw Zaqar he sighed and sat on my hood. "She's an alcoholic," he said, and I said, "No shit," and he just looked at me like I was the problem and said, "It's a disease. Man, she can't stop. She told me." He shook his head. "Just like my uncle," he said. "Broke my heart."

When Omar opened the passenger door, a sour vomit smell came out, which made me really angry. "I'm calling the cops," I said, and Omar put a hand out and said, "Hold up," and then he got Bubby on his walkie-talkie, like they'd made some kind of arrangement beforehand.

Not much later, Bubby drove up in his beat-up Caddy, and he and Omar got Zaqar, half conscious, in the backseat. I helped. She grabbed my shirt for a second and pulled me close, and I thought she might spit in my face, but she said, "If I were fictional, people would love me. But I'm real. I'm real! I'm a person, and so everyone hates me." I shook my head and got away from her grip. Her smell made me gag.

I found out later that Omar and Bubby took her to Carrows and bought her a stack of pancakes. The restaurant made them eat outside near the garbage bins so that Zaqar wouldn't disturb the customers.

AT ABOUT THIS point in my story, the cell phone on Father Bill's desk rang and shook, startling us both. Father Bill didn't answer, muting the ringtone. He got up and kinked the blinds with his fingers, peeking through. A couple of potted cactuses were on the windowsill. He stretched his neck by tilting his head right, then left. Then he sat back down.

I told him that for a few days after that, all I wanted to do was sleep, and I couldn't stop dreaming about Zaqar. In one dream, she was like a fish, opening her mouth, then closing it, then opening it again. In another, it was more of a feeling like in the past, begging God to make me fall out of love with Zaqar or to make her stop drinking. I didn't care which, just as long as one of them happened, and I got relief. I remembered her walking down the sidewalk to meet me outside a movie theater, and how the air around her seemed to light up. She would make me laugh so hard by pretending to be stupid, saying in this hillbilly voice, "What, what, what?" after I said something academic- or intellectual-sounding. Then I remembered her calling me maybe a few months before she showed up in my office and telling me that she hadn't been faithful. She was crying a little. I said, "This is the first time you've been honest with me." And she said, "I know, because I'm drunk." She asked if I'd still be her friend. She said she wished she could find a way to drink without hurting herself or anyone else. She wanted to be a good person—it was just too hard. She couldn't do it. "Drinking is the only thing that helps." Before she hung up, she asked, "Am I doomed?"

The next afternoon, after my fiction workshop, I called Omar and asked him to help me find Zaqar. I felt ashamed. I didn't know what I was going to do, but I wanted to try to do something. Omar and I waited until his shift ended, and then in a smog-enhanced sunset, he drove me around Los Angeles in his Camry. He opened his glove box and one-handedly lit a joint, telling me not to worry, that he had a medical-marijuana license for anxiety. He was about the least anxious person I knew, and I told him so. "Medicine doing its job, I suppose," he said with a cool smile.

The sunset looked postapocalyptic, and the zombie-like druggies and crazies and homeless people sleeping and wandering and leaning against walls didn't help. When we got to Zaqar's alleyway, Omar asked me what made me change my mind, and why I wanted to help Zaqar now. "I don't know," I said. He said his uncle was his favorite person in the world, even if he took his own life with drink. His eyes welled up and he wiped them with his forearm.

Zaqar was in another alleyway behind a liquor store, near where Omar had dropped her off before. She had passed out in some dirty blankets and clothes and towels, and we shook her for a long time before she opened her eyes. She smelled like rancid honey. Her skin was very pink, almost the color of a rash. I got really scared when she looked at me—her eyes a sickly yellow—and said, "Who are you?" She had a bagged bottle beside her, and Omar picked it up, sniffed, and she reached her hand out, so he passed it to her. She drank, but there wasn't much left. Omar said,

"Honey, let's try to get you some help," and she shook her head. She put her hands on her bloated liver and ignored us after that, lying back down in her blanket pile.

Omar and I conversed for a few minutes, and he told me that the hospitals wouldn't take her; he'd tried before. A man in a tight fetal position shook in the corner. Near him was a patrolling cop who seemed bored or used to it all.

I fished in my pockets and pulled out a couple of twenties and my billiard-ball key chain with keys for my office and my Volvo. I went to my knees so that I could look Zaqar in the eyes, and I put her hand out and set these items in her palm. She blinked and then she stared at me like she'd expected nothing from me and I'd exceeded her hopes.

On the drive back to campus, Omar played some R&B on low volume and hummed to it. I had an extra set of keys in my office, and Omar had to open the door for me with his skeleton key. He said, "It's not like she needs your permission. But she'll take it as a sign. She'll come back now for sure."

I STOPPED TALKING and Father Bill leaned forward. "Did she come back?" he asked. I shook my head and said, "It's been more than two weeks. We've looked. She's nowhere." I choked back a sob. "Sorry," I said. "I cry all the time. Pray all the time. It's like I'm reaching around in the dark, trying to feel for something solid."

Father Bill leaned back and stretched his legs to unearth a wrinkled package of Merits from his pocket, along with a Bic lighter, and he lit one and regarded me while he smoked. He got about halfway done and smashed it out in a paper cup. Then he said that I was in that space he'd told me about when we'd first met—that expansiveness—and that the best thing I could do was be all the way inside it. "I should have helped her," I told him, and Father Bill looked me right in the eyes and said that there wasn't anything more to be done. Then he paused, as if preparing me for what he had to say next. He spoke quietly, an emotional tremor in his voice. He said that Zaqar knew I loved her, which was why she had come to me. He was sure of it, and she loved me, too. We were wrong for each other, of course; that was evident, he said, but neither one of us could do anything about it.

ABOUT A WEEK after my talk with Father Bill, my Volvo disappeared from the parking lot. I knew it was Zaqar. My fiction class had ended, and I went to the tree I'd parked beneath and sat with my back against its trunk. The breeze shook the tree leaves every few seconds or so, as if a wave had gone over them, their silvery undersides shimmering.

About ten minutes later, Omar buzzed up in his cart, some trash cans rattling in the back. "You got insurance for theft?" he said, squinting in the sun. I put my head in my hands. Omar came and sat next to me, and I felt an arm around my shoulder. I glanced at his face, at his eyes shining with sadness. "Sorry, son," he said. He told me that he had connections with the police department and that he'd keep an ear for news.

Two nights later my cell phone rang at home. I went outside to the backyard to answer. Omar told me that the police had found Zaqar's body in my Volvo parked at a private beach in Malibu. I couldn't say anything for a few minutes. I looked for the moon but couldn't find it—the stars veiled and muted behind clouds in the huge expanse of sky. "Did she hurt anyone?" I asked. "Was she drunk?" He told me no, she hadn't hurt anyone, and yes, she'd been drunk, and that she'd died from it, just like his uncle had. I couldn't help Zaqar—couldn't do anything—but I'd tried anyway, and now I'm painfully aware. I feel too alive. Zaqar demanded nothing less from me. Omar said if I needed anything to let him know, and I thanked him. After we hung up, I stayed outside for a while and listened to the crickets and the wind in the trees and the low cheery chatter and music of TVs in the houses around me. I imagined Zaqar picking a private beach near a movie star's mansion, finding her spot, rolling down the windows, and lying back in the car seat, the waves shushing and misting the air, releasing her.

PARIS

Roxanne Flick's industrious great-grandfather built the house along Newport Bay. Now it's worth millions. With characteristic self-effacing irony, Roxy calls the house "the beach shack," and a sun-bleached driftwood sign with this title festoons the front door. The Flicks had been wealthy and influential but then experienced a drastic generational decline in fortune. Roxy's own mother and uncle squandered millions on lawyers, fighting over their indeterminate inheritance, amassed mostly in the beach shack, which Roxy's uncle won though a court settlement. But late one night, intoxicated and wandering the marine-fogged street in his boxers, he fell and hit his head on the curbside, bleeding to death. Roxy's uncle had no heirs, and so the beach shack went to her mother.

Nick finishes regaling his girlfriend Lara with this summarized version of his ex-wife's family's history. They're almost at the beach shack now. Yesterday his former mother-in-law had a massive stroke. Roxy has asked him to stop by and get apprised of the situation. Having punched in the uninspired security code, 1111, he waits for the gate to crank open, and then he slowly drives his Mercedes down Bay Side Private Road. Outside the windshield, the sun looks like a brass ball slung between two palm trees. "It's the men," he explains to Lara, "who usually die. Badly, violently. My former mother-in-law—I still call her Mom—went through four. The last one had a rear-ender on the 405 South. He got out of his car and was walking to the freeway shoulder when a big truck flattened him. Roxy's brother died young: drugs. But the women are indestructible. It's like some witchcraft-type thing. I got out with my life. I shit you not. Had I stayed married to Roxy"—one hand on the steering wheel, he slits his finger alongside his throat with his other.

Lara smiles with chagrined amusement. Twenty-three years younger than his fifty-two years, she wears horn-rimmed glasses (nonprescription, she says they make her "look smart") and has a soothing voice. Sometimes he has to ask her to speak up. Her long brown hair is lighter at the ends and around her face. She's an interior decorator and she also gives watercolor lessons.

"Roxy loves the beach shack," Nick says. "It'll be hers after Mom dies. The older the Flick women get," he adds, parking in the brick driveway, "the scarier they are." He cuts the ignition.

"It's not PC to say, but it's true. Menopause is the final straw. Men become irrelevant. Roxy's let herself go. If you ask me, it's sad."

"It's also brave," says Lara. "Beauty standards for women are crazy in SoCal." She's originally from Minnesota and likes to remind him.

"Sure," says Nick. "Such courage."

As they walk to the front door Lara says, "Have you heard of the Kardashian curse?"

"I don't watch that shit," he says. "But let me guess: the men get life-fucked and the women dominate."

"Female energy," she agrees, "has overtaken that family."

"It's the same with the Flicks," he says.

Constructed of massive whitewashed walls around a heavily foliaged and shaded courtyard, the beach shack has large picture windows overlooking the bay. A heavy wood door studded with brass gives way to the courtyard, where a winged cherub at the center of a clamshell fountain sprays water from the palms of its extended chubby hands.

The doorbell barely rings, so Nick knocks. Roxy answers, and after introductions he tells her that she has to get the doorbell fixed. She laughs and says, "He thinks he's still my husband." Married for twenty years, they've been separated coming on five. Both their kids are away at college. She turns her attention to him and says, "I don't *have to* do anything, but thank you, sir, for your input." The rhythmical splash of the fountain sounds like laughter. With resentment, he regards her: Barefoot, she wears loose jeans—mom jeans. Her middle has thickened, and there's a puffiness around her groin area. She isn't wearing a bra, her breasts swinging inside her T-shirt, and her gray braid falls across her shoulder. She leads them through the courtyard, saying, "Mom took a turn. 'This might be it,' the nurse says. 'Days, hours, minutes. Who knows?'"

This was supposed to be a quick visit: Nick and Lara have a date planned. But now he'll have to make a trip to the hospital in case Mom dies. "I should see her," he says, "but I'd like to bring tulips." Mom's favorite flower. "I should've thought of it earlier."

"There's no rush," Roxy says, adding, "Mom's not going to die in the next few hours—I don't care what that nurse says."

Nick looks at Lara and she nods. He glances appraisingly at her breasts: rounded, modest, fake.

"Mom loves Nick more than me," Roxy says to Lara. "It's in her blood. She prefers men. She calls him 'my little man.'"

"Not after I told her to stop," he says.

"She still does," she says. "When you're not around." She guides them to the living room, where a leather couch faces the picture windows. The water is sparkly and bright outside, boats bobbing at their docks, and Nick notices a skeletal osprey perched on the pier.

Roxy asks if Lara wants a tour. Of course she does, thinks Nick. They amble through the rooms, up the stairs, back down. Everything looks old, and whatever is new has been created to look old, giving the façade of English antiquity and nobility. The bedrooms have massive canopied bed frames, and the walls are hung with tapestries of foxhunts and landscapes. The bathrooms have claw-footed tubs and chain-pull toilets. There are four tomb-like fireplaces.

Lara is practiced in the art of being impressed, and her appreciative interior-decorator commentary brings pleasure to Roxy, her cheeks reddening.

When the tour is finished, Lara says, "I love your home, I really do. You've done a beautiful job."

Roxy says, "We'd be quite rich if it weren't for everything we do to keep up. Mom and I are working on a book." She nods toward the stacks of papers and a laptop on the dining room table. "I'll have to finish on my own now. It's about some of the more famous people who've lived in Newport connected to our family: John Wayne, who was a friend of Poppy's. Did you know his daughter owns a spin studio called True Grit? I'm too afraid to take a class! Also Todd something-or-other, I can't ever remember his last name. Starts with an *M*. The disgraced football player. Cops recently found him naked and huddled in someone's backyard with a paper bag filled with meth. Poppy also knew his granddad, and his dad was a big-time football coach who trained Todd from a baby to be a super athlete. He'd throw raw steak into Todd's playpen for him to gnaw on when he was teething."

Todd *Marinovich*, Nick thinks as he says, "We should get going."

Roxy says, "That's code for stop talking. I'm embarrassing him." She lifts and stretches, the skin under her arms flappy, her eyes glimmering. "You forget," she says, "that I know you better than you know yourself."

"You think," he says, "you know me. But you don't."

"I'll change clothes," Roxy says, heading for the stairway.

Nick wishes he could tell her to put on a bra, and then she calls back, "Don't worry, Nick. I'll put on a brassiere."

Nick says to Lara, "She likes to make me uncomfortable. Some things never change. For a while I called her Bush. She thought I was teasing her because she wasn't a fan of W and his father.

But it was because"—he motions toward his pelvic area—"she refused to take care of her business down there. She was devastated by our separation. Still is."

Lara nods solemnly.

Roxy comes down the stairs in a turquoise velour jumpsuit. It looks like something Mom would wear. He notices her upper body is now secured.

A caretaker is wheeling the Flicks' longtime neighbor in a wheelchair along the pier next door. Howard, a looming, tall, cigar-smoking retired CEO, has lived next to the beach shack for as long as Nick can remember. As an aspiring businessman, Nick had always wanted to tap the source. Yet Howard inevitably directed the subject matter. Their most extensive conversation had been about a successful procedure Howard had undergone to have his hemorrhoids removed. Regardless, Nick always felt a strong admiration.

Nick decides to say hello to Howard. He goes out the side door and then opens the gate that partitions the homes and piers. The afternoon sun is sharp-rimmed and there's a soft breeze. It's low tide, and the glittery bay water slaps and sweeps back in gentle little waves. A bell buoy dings in the distance. The caretaker—possibly Chinese or Vietnamese—is diminutive and feminine with dark bangs. He approaches and greets her, explaining that he's an old friend. Unsmiling, she nods and moves aside so that he can speak directly to Howard, who is forlorn and thin and almost entirely lost in a thick woolen blanket, his colorless wrinkled forehead and wide scared eyes peeking out, mouth covered. Nick bends to Howard's ear. "Hey, buddy," he says. Howard's eyes alter, becoming less scared. A grunt comes from the blanket.

Nick glances toward the beach shack, where Roxy's and Lara's faces watch from the window like dots. Another grunt comes from the blanket and Nick pulls in closer. He's not sure what to say or do. Should he tell Howard that he's risen in his company to become the top sales consultant? No. This won't impress a CEO. He feels for his cell phone in his jacket pocket and pulls it out. Knowing Roxy and Lara are watching, he crouches lower, his cell phone cupped in his hand, and scrolls through his photos of the women he's dated (including a bikini shot of Lara). Howard grunts and then he makes a strange bubbling noise. His mouth arises from the blanket and he smiles like a baby.

WHEN NICK RETURNS, he's pensive. They decide that Roxy and Nick will go to the hospital and Lara will wait at the beach shack. Roxy opens a bottle of Chardonnay for Lara and tells her to make herself at home. Before they leave, Roxy makes sure Lara knows how to work the cable and Blu-ray player. She has to explain twice. Afterward Roxy turns her eyes to Nick, so Lara can't see. Lara may be pretty, her hidden expression says, but she's not bright. Nick has the urge to smear her face with his hand.

BEFORE THEY GO to the hospital, Nick gives Roxy cash to buy a bouquet of yellow-tipped tulips for Mom at the local outdoor flower bodega. Roxy knows the owners, so it makes sense for her to buy the flowers, and now she chats with one of them while Nick waits. Spindly-looking tables and chairs are set around the bodega, and a woman at one of the tables curses while playing a computerized chess game, then glares at her coughing male companion. They're eighty-something and wear matching checkered golf sweaters. The man puts a crumpled Kleenex to his mouth and gives Nick a beseeching look. Nick turns his back to the couple. A fat man wearing a straw hat tells two Latino employees that he loves this place, that it's the closest you can come in Newport Beach to Paris. Then he asks, "Have you ever been to Paris?" and the employees shake their heads no.

At a stoplight near the hospital Nick says, "I saw you watching me with Howard." The light changes and he drives, saying, "You want to see what I showed him?"

Roxy shakes her head no like the flower bodega employees.

ABOVE MOM'S HOSPITAL bed is a fake skylight lit with adjustable skies: morning, day, starry night. Fat, lovely clouds drift across its blue surface.

Mom is propped in a sitting position, sleeping with a breathing tube down her throat, multiple IVs stuck in her arms. Her eyelids are swollen, the eyelashes poking out. Nick waits while Roxy, chummy and familiar with the nurses, drops a box of See's chocolates at the nurses' station. When she returns Nick says, "Don't wake her," but Roxy has already moved forward to squeeze Mom's forearm, saying, "Mommy? You've got a special visitor, Mommy."

Mom's eyes open and stare at Nick. Her look shocks him, holding nothing back, and then she blinks and he comes forward woozily and holds her hand. She tightens her grip and strokes him with her thumb, and he begins to cry. Roxy moves behind them. He hears her say, "Mommy, do you know who this is? Who is he, Mommy?"

Mom beams at Nick. Her eyes say: My little man. Even after his affairs and the divorce, Mom still loves him.

He glances at Roxy and her face shines. She places her purse on the bedside tray next to the tulips and moves to him, embracing him for the first time in years. Her bulky body presses against his, and his heart pulses. For reasons he doesn't understand, his cock stiffens. He shifts his weight and pulls his hips outward, hoping Roxy hasn't noticed.

BACK FROM THE hospital, Roxy and Nick watch Lara from the beach shack's picture window: On the dock at the end of the pier, she sits looking out at the sunset, her bare feet dipped in the polluted bay water, her high heels next to her, a wide-bottomed glass of Chardonnay palmed in an outstretched hand, and her hair flapping in the breeze. Nick likes how she looks casual and sexy. She could be in an advertisement for Viagra or mutual funds. The sun is down but it's still light, a long pink spray across the skyline, and overhead a mottled half moon the dirty white of cauliflower.

Roxy says, "How does she wear those heels and not fall?"

Nick roots in his pocket and unearths his cell phone. Scrolling through the photos of his women, he says, "Howard's a good man."

"Put that away," Roxy says, giving him a dismissive hand wave.

He pockets his cell and leans back on the couch, closing his eyes.

•

ROXY TREATS NICK and Lara to dinner that night at the Newport Yacht Club. Nick knows it's the best way for her to use Mom's free membership dining points by the end of the month. She sits across from them in a booth. The room is dimly lit with a centerpiece fireplace; a jazz trio tinkers near the bar, and multiple televisions play golf and football on mute, closed captioning striped across the bottoms of their screens. (Nick reads: *He could certainly use a birdie*.) An older white crowd with lots of walkers and canes, rich pinched faces, enter and dine and leave, accompanied by equally unhappy younger versions with genetically similar bodies and faces.

The food is heavy and tasteless. Lara seems strangely vacant, fiddling with a deep-fried artichoke heart that looks like a fuzzy ear. Nick texts Shell under the table. Her name's Shellie, but she goes by Shell. He notices Lara catching the light of his cell phone, so he quickly puts it in his pocket; then he scoots and lifts himself from the booth. "Restroom?" he asks, and Roxy points the direction, though she knows he knows where it is and her face shows this to him.

Nick goes to the dark hall near the bathroom and calls Shell, watching Roxy and Lara to make sure they don't follow. Lara's face in the dim light reminds Nick of a statue. The phone rings and goes to Shell's voice mail. He texts: *Let's meet*. Shell is younger than Lara and not as insecure. On the nearby TV, six pretty girls in various-colored bras and panties and feather headdresses, arms at each other's shoulders, move in a leg-crossing strut, their hips thrust forward. Roxy, he sees now, has spotted him. Their eyes meet and she rakes him with contempt. He disappears into the shadow of the hall. "Busted," he says to no one.

A WEEK LATER, Nick stops by the beach shack after a trip to the hospital. It's past seven and dark out, a half dozen stars peppering the sky and a moon like polished steel. Despite the prognoses, Mom has not died. He visits more than Roxy now, but Mom is comatose and doesn't know the difference.

Roxy hasn't fixed the doorbell. The air is still, and he hears the murmuring bay and the distant whirring from a neighbor's sprinkler. Roxy answers and tells him her book club is meeting, so he can't stay. He twists and pulls Mom's wedding band—a simple thin gold ring—off his pinkie finger and then hands it to her, explaining: "I couldn't get it off Mom's swelled finger. No one could. Then this nurse saves the day, so we don't have to cut the ring off. He pulls a loose thread from my shirt and wraps it around her finger at the knuckle, and the blood back-gorges. He says it's painful, but Mom doesn't wince. Then he slides the ring over the string and pulls it off, and wa-la."

She says, "How's Lara?"

"I'm with someone new." He'd meant his words to sound light and playful, but they seem strangely intense.

"Not a surprise," she says.

Nick knows Roxy won't wear the ring. She'll probably put it in the kitchen junk drawer with the old keys, stray batteries, and other useless and forgotten miscellanea. But it doesn't matter. Whether she wants him or not, he's hers.

LOWLIFE

George wants a divorce. We'll share custody, he says. He's got this idea that it'll be simple and relatively painless, like that pretentious bitch with her conscious uncoupling. Danny is fourteen and obsessed with hip-hop. The other day his eyes were red, so I straight out asked if he'd been smoking pot. He said no, no he hadn't, and that some of his friends do, but not him, and that his eyes just get this way sometimes. I said would you tell me if you were. He said no, no he wouldn't. George says I'm overreacting and that Danny's on the soccer team and doing well in school, which is true. George helps coach and he's interested in Team Mom, who also attends the games and practices. The team's not that good, but somehow they've made the playoffs.

"I don't have time for your jealousy," George said, when I finally confronted him about Team Mom. He was talking from his cell phone at a Costco, buying two cases of Gatorade. His voice sounded different, and the background noise made it seem like he was at the airport. He joined a gym, lost weight, started wearing nicer clothes, and bought a new cell phone. I'm sure Danny notices. He told me once that he likes Team Mom, that she's cool. I wear my mirrored sunglasses and closely watch her and George at Danny's games. She's taller, younger, and prettier than I am.

Danny plays music for me in the minivan and we drive all over our city, Tucson. This is when I feel closest to him. He has an extension cord and he picks songs from his iPod. Sometimes he sings along. "Have you heard that lowlife song?" I asked the other day, knowing he had. I sang the lyric: "'I'm always rapping for the lowlife—lowlife, lowlife, lowlife.'"

Danny gave me a look that said the song was overplayed and overrated. Then he said, "It's 'repping,' not 'rapping.' Repping for the lowlife."

"Like representing?"

He shrug-nodded.

THAT WEEKEND I missed the playoffs because I had to fly to Orange County for my mom, who still lives in Newport Beach in the home I grew up in. Her husband had died the month before. No funeral—she'd already scattered his ashes over the Pacific—but she needed me for what she termed a Celebration of Life. "It's not an option," she'd told my brother and me about attending. Yet my brother managed to use a moneymaking business trip as an excuse.

Mom had been married to Manning Smith—her third husband—for twelve years, and he'd left her three times in the last five for his mistress, but he always came back. When Mom wasn't blaming the slut mistress for Manning's infidelities, she blamed a fall: Manning had tripped coming to bed. "It's a brain injury," she'd say. "The brain is very complicated." But I'll testify that he was an asshole long before that.

Mom was putting off hip-replacement surgery, and she strategically veered from wall to table to couch to sit. It reminded me of how Danny would toddle between George and me when he first started walking.

The life celebration was at a Ruth's Chris Steak House. Mom wore a bright floral silk pantsuit and she looked stunning, her diamond ring, earrings, and necklace flashing. Her hair had been cut short and styled and looked like the flame from a struck match. She stood in the same spot for most of the afternoon and let people come to her, so that they wouldn't notice her hip problem.

My stick-thin aunt bombarded me with her alcohol-and-cigarette breath, telling me that I was heavier but otherwise looked the same. Thanks and fuck you, too, I said in my head. My relatives took advantage along with the other guests, eating steaks as big as their heads and drinking as much as they could on Mom's dime. It was like Manning Smith was alive again, leeching off my mom. A staticky microphone got passed so that stories could be mumbled about Manning, mostly from plump old red-faced men, bragging about their golfing glory days.

Manning's mistress had threatened to crash the celebration, so Mom's hairdresser, Neil, a brown belt in karate, stood guard outside in the sunshine near the valets. The mistress didn't show, but she called pretending to be me. The hostess approached my mom and said that "a Millicent" was on the phone and wanted to speak to her. "I'm Millicent," I said, "so"—I gestured to the phone—"she's a liar."

Though we'd both had a couple of drinks, Mom drove us home in her Porsche when the celebration ended. She clipped a parked Mercedes with her side mirror on the narrow street near her house, but we pretended not to notice.

After we'd showered and changed into pajamas, we met at the couch in the living room and sat quietly. She pressed a wadded Kleenex to her eyes, mopping a few tears, and then she looked at me and said, "That certainly went well," and I vigorously agreed.

After a long silence she said that she'd gotten blood taken at the doctor's and that the woman who took her blood also knew Manning, because of all his health problems. He'd been so friendly, Mom added, perking up, lots of people liked him, and then she got sad and low-voiced again, saying she'd told the woman who took her blood that Manning had passed away, and then the blood woman had asked, Who's that other woman who comes in with him? meaning, of course, the slut mistress. And the same thing had happened at the gas station: she'd told the gas guy that Manning died, and then the gas guy also asked about the woman, was it Manning's daughter? Mom looked sad, tired, and humiliated, and I said that that must've been rough, and she nodded grimly and said, "It'll happen again. It's not over."

She told me the slut mistress ruined her life and I said, "It takes two, Mom," because I hated Manning and he deserved blame. But then I regretted having spoken, because her eyes radiated and shone with his betrayal, the hurt boundless.

We were quiet for a long time, our thoughts ricocheting, and then she said that she'd recently heard—she didn't know where—that the four things a person regrets not having said after a loved one dies are: one, "I forgive you"; two, "I hope you forgive me"; and three, "I love you."

"What's the fourth?" I asked.

She looked bewildered.

"Maybe it's just three things," I said.

THE NEXT MORNING Mom was up early, wearing a frilly white-and-pink tennis skirt with matching shoes, though her playing days had ceased because of her hip. I'd already had coffee and breakfast. Mom didn't believe in breakfast or lunch; she barely ate, and not until late in the day. A taped tennis match played loudly on the living room television screen, the *pock* of balls and the moaning and grunting players our familiar background sound. She steered herself along the wall, leading me slowly down the same hallway I'd loved to sock-slide as a kid, to an empty back room where I used to do my high school homework. She spoke as if to herself, saying, "Too much, too much." She motioned with her hand for me to go past her—she hated my having to wait for her—so I did.

I opened the door, and it was like walking into the history of my brother and me. Our mission projects from grade school were set up on the bureau. I remembered burning myself with the glue gun, and I ran a finger down the scar between my thumb and forefinger. My giant-headed aluminum Prince tennis racquet was on a chair, and I picked it up and did a practice swing. On the desk, I saw yellowing term papers and a file full of report cards. I fingered some lumpy envelopes filled with our childhood teeth. My face warmed as I thumbed through an essay I'd written about how marriage was another form of prostitution, which, I saw now, had received a B minus, the teacher scribbling along the side, *Thought-provoking and passionate, but needs more research! Back your claims!* The closet door was cracked open, and the closest floor was stacked with folded baby and childhood clothes. I recognized a dress patterned with sunflowers that I used to love, since it matched my mom's dress. I peeked into the closet and saw the lace of my wedding gown, tucked behind a thick plastic armor. "Jesus, Mom," I said. "You saved everything?"

She sighed and said, "I made Manning take it all down from the attic. I've been trying to sort though it, but it's too much."

I glanced at my wedding gown again. I vaguely remembered Mom offering to have it cleaned and stored. When we'd gone shopping for the dress, Mom and I had argued, and it was the concession dress: both conservative (for Mom) and sexy (for me) with a low-cut bodice. The price, she'd told me at the time, didn't matter. You only get married once, she'd said. If you're lucky.

It occurred to me that she should move—the house and everything inside weighty with memories—and I said, "Throw everything away, Mom."

She was silent for a long time. Then she said, "There's Seagram's wine coolers in the fridge. You used to like those. I think I'll have one now."

"It isn't even noon," I said.

"Well," she said, "like my uncle Fred used to say: 'It doesn't matter, don't think twice, lift your skirt and slide on the ice.'"

"God, Mom," I said. "Didn't Uncle Fred commit tax fraud?"

She leaned her back against the wall and peered at me. "Millicent," she said. "Why does George want a divorce?"

"God, Mom."

She waited.

I babbled. He's become distant and preoccupied. It's a midlife thing. I didn't tell her that George would say my hypersensitivity, anxiety, and erratic behaviors are problems, along with my constant dissatisfaction. I talked about how I'd taken up yoga. Then I heard myself say, "It won't be so bad. Like conscious uncoupling."

"Speak English," she said, and then repeated: "Why divorce?"

I didn't say, It's Team Mom—younger, sexier—but it showed in my eyes, and I stared hard at her until she looked down and said, "Well, that's that."

My cell buzzed in my pocket. I answered because it was Danny.

"Hey," he said, "how's Grandma?"

"She's right here," I said, and I passed her the phone.

She beamed while she talked—yes-and-no answers, asking about his school, small-talking about the weather—and there was a long pause and her eyes welled and she said, "I love you, too, so much, so much, you can't imagine, Danny," and too overcome to speak more, she passed back my phone.

"Is she okay?" Danny asked.

Mom raised her hand, and I said, "She's fine," and then I asked about his playoff game. Mom began slowly making her way down the hallway, and I followed.

"We won," he said. "One to zero. We're in the finals."

"That's great!"

"I made the goal. But the ball accidentally bounced off my leg."

"That counts," I said.

"Whatever, Mom. It bounced off me. That's not why I called. Jenna pierced my ear."

"What?"

"It's infected, Mom."

My mom, in the kitchen, was having trouble screwing the cap off a wine cooler. She glanced at me and I mimed the motion of opening with a bottle opener.

"It hurts," he said. "There's, like, pus, and it's red and swollen."

"Who's Jenna?" I asked.

He ignored me, saying, "Mom, it looks bad. I want both ears pierced. But, God, Mom, it hurt. I don't want to tell Dad."

"Who's Jenna?"

"*Jenna*," he stressed.

"Jennifer," I said, remembering. "She's smart. I like her." I'd known her since she and Danny were in kindergarten. She used to call me Milli-Mommy instead of Millicent, and she'd had a passion for dolphins in the second grade. By the sixth, she'd insisted on being called Jenna. "Why'd she pierce your ear?"

He didn't respond.

"Is she one of your friends who smokes pot?"

He snort-laughed and then said, "Mom, no."

I felt coldness on my bicep and realized it was Mom passing me a Peach Fuzzy Navel wine cooler. I took it from her and told Danny to find his dad, because I needed to speak to him.

George and I talked, and he agreed to take a look at Danny's ear. My mom wasn't listening—watching the tennis match and sucking on her wine cooler—so I asked George if he and Team Mom had celebrated the playoff victory.

"Jesus, Millie, let it go."

"Did you?"

"Of course not."

I didn't say anything, stifling a burp.

"Listen," he said, his voice softening, "give your mom my love. I'll see you soon."

"How could you?" I said, and then I said Team Mom's name. He exhaled.

I hung up and then said, "Fuck you."

My mom looked over from the couch and I pretended to still be in conversation, pausing to whisper to her, "It's George. I'll go in the other room," and she nodded eagerly and said, "Take your time!"

I took the remaining coolers and the bottle opener—cell phone propped between my ear and shoulder—and Mom said, "There's a pack of Benson & Hedges and a lighter in the guest bathroom drawer. Take your time!"

In the memory museum, I drank, smoked stale cigarettes, and looked and remembered until the late afternoon. A few tears unloaded, but I didn't allow myself a full sob. I unzipped the plastic armor and fingered my wedding gown, then took it out and laid it across the desk, ashing on the pearled bodice. It wouldn't fit anymore, and I thought of my aunt saying I was heavier but otherwise the same. Buzzed from the coolers and nicotine, I called George again. He didn't answer, so I texted him a string of meaningless emojis, including my favorite: what I think of as the Rodin-thinking-fist-at-chin face.

After some time I felt bad about the ash, so I opened the window and screen and flopped the wedding dress out, shaking it. It loosened from my grip and fell in a lump on the water heater and shrub below. Ha, I thought. Good riddance.

When I came back to the living room, I saw that Mom, on the couch watching golf now and picking at a leftover cheese platter from the celebration, had changed to a bright blue tracksuit. She looked fragile and grief-stricken, her hair slicked and her face expectant and shiny with lotion. I sat next to her and took a breath and said, "We're going to work it out. We're not divorcing."

She startled me, swinging one clenched fist upward in a victory salute, saying, "Oh, Millicent, I'm so pleased! I knew it! I just knew it!"

She opened her arms wide and I went in, squeezing my eyes shut. In the blackness of my eyelids and for the duration of our hug, I assured myself that I was merely stretching the truth. But when she released me and I opened my eyes to the brightness of her face, I felt despair. I couldn't compete with Team Mom, nor should I have to, nor did I want to. But I kept my face blank and happy, mimicking Mom's expression, and then she said, "Let's celebrate!"

We uncorked one of Manning's bottles of wine and ordered in Chinese, which we both left mostly untouched. Mom got sleepy-eyed during a CNN documentary on the eighties, so we said goodnight early. I watched her list against the wall, pigeon-toed and with a heart-shaped backside, down the hallway to her room.

In bed I texted with Danny for a few minutes. They'd been creamed in the finals, zero to seven, but Danny didn't mind, he was glad it was over. His dad had taken out his earring and cleaned the piercing, and it felt better. They'd recheck it in the morning. *Goodnight LL*, he texted. *Love you*. I didn't know what he meant but didn't ask, texting back: *Love you too. Goodnight.* In that hazy space before sleep, I recognized *LL* meant "lowlife."

AT ABOUT THREE in the morning, I bolted awake, remembering my wedding dress. I went to the window and saw the ghostly white gleam, hanging spiderweb-like between a bush and the water heater, an edge flapping in the breeze. I tried to pull it in with one of my brother's fishing rods, but it was heavy and kept sliding off.

So I went out the front door and down the side of the house, sidling my way through the shrubs, a motion-sensor light suddenly spotlighting me, and then I was gripping the silky material, damp now with dew. Heaving it like a dead lamb around my shoulders, I brought it inside. I set it flat along the floor—Jesus-like with sleeves akimbo—and stared for a long time, feeling both nostalgic and horrified. After smoothing my hands over the rustling length, I reinserted the dress in its thick plastic sheath and placed the whole thing on its puffy hanger, deep and hidden in the closet where it belongs.

Dogs

For over a month Jackie had been meeting Susan at the baseball field after the high school team practiced to let their dogs play in the dusk, the stadium lights still buzzing (timed to go off an hour and a half later), the night air and small talk a pleasant distraction. Then a few weeks ago Kent had showed up with his dog, and after that he started meeting them, too. They'd not known each other beforehand and converged by happenstance. All they had in common was the dogs. When Jackie would arrive before Kent, she'd notice how, while chitchatting, Susan would keep an eye on the outfield and entrance gate.

Tootsie wasn't even Jackie's dog—he belonged to Douglas. But Douglas rarely walked Tootsie. Jackie knew it would be the same with the baby—her responsibility. Eight months pregnant, she sat on the dugout bench, her hands resting on the dome of her stomach, and watched Kent and Susan jog, the dogs leaping and laughing between them, tongues dangling and tails slashing. It bothered her that Tootsie couldn't keep up. He lagged behind, tottering on stubby legs, a freakish-looking shelter mutt whom Douglas had saved from certain extermination almost three years earlier, an orange-brown color with a head far too large for his body.

On their third lap, something about the synchronicity of Kent's and Susan's legs made Jackie wonder if they'd begun a sexual relationship. For some reason, she felt betrayed. Hormones, she decided. It wasn't like she really knew these people or cared about them. She was becoming more sensitive and daydreamy as her pregnancy progressed; she didn't know what she wanted anymore. Douglas had been pestering her to marry him these last few weeks, each morning saying: "It's a ten-minute drive to the courthouse."

A full moon was low in the sky, and Jackie watched as Kent and Susan finished, the dogs panting, pacing, and smiling. Her fists at her hips, Susan moved from one leg to the other, catching her breath, while Fozzie Bear, her purebred golden retriever, plopped his body down in the grass. The oldest at thirty-four, Susan would talk openly and bitterly about her ongoing divorce battle, especially if prompted. Yet she had a sluggish, melancholic expression that appealed to Jackie and seemed associated with vulnerability; it never fully left her face, even when she smiled or laughed. Jackie knew that she was from somewhere in the Midwest and that she worked at some financial something-or-other business, as did her soon-to-be ex. Her long hair was highlighted the same gold-wheat-blond as her dog's fur, and Jackie thought Fozzie's carefree warmth reflected what Susan might be more like if she weren't so guarded and angry.

Kent reached for a tennis ball in the pocket of his nylon jacket, and then he whipped the ball toward the outfield, the dogs sprinting after it, Tootsie shambling behind. Jackie had waited on men like Kent and found them attractive: they spoke about everything with irony—even ordered their food in a joking manner; and their facial expressions, including their resting faces, always had a twinkle of sarcasm. She couldn't imagine being able to laugh at everything. But she noticed that with the dogs Kent became earnest, squatting to stroke their fur and whisper in their ears. Like Jackie, he was twenty-three, but unlike her, he seemed to have a limitless future; he'd show up at the field looking—depending on what he wore—like different men, as if his very being contained boundless potentials: hooded sweatshirts or preppy clothes or business attire or arty shirts or surfer shorts or exercise gear like now; she thought of him secretly as Chameleon Kent. Though his background was sketchy and he didn't talk much, she'd gleaned that his wealthy adoptive parents lived nearby and that he was considering grad school in business. He kept his thick brown hair very short and without a part and he had a low widow's peak like Dracula. Cher, his sleek black-Lab mix, was the alpha dog, often humping Tootsie and Fozzie. They laughed and joked that Cher was hypersexual, but really the dog had a manic, disturbing energy.

Cher had the ball (she always got it) and the dogs ran back to Kent, Tootsie far behind. The klieg-like stadium lights made it seem like they were all playing their parts in a movie, and Jackie had the urge to shout: "I know you're fucking!" Then she watched Kent bending to place his mouth to Susan's lips. Their heads came apart, and as if sensing Jackie's stare, they both looked at her. Heat spread at her neck and cheeks and around her eyes.

"Oh," Susan said, moving from Kent and smiling.

"Hey, sorry," Kent said. "We forgot about you."

"You're so quiet," Susan added.

Ever since childhood Jackie had been embarrassed to be the center of attention, especially when she didn't know what she was feeling, and this hadn't changed. She turned away on the bench but couldn't hide her discomfort. Her cheeks blazed. "Tootsie!" she called, and when his warm body sidled against her legs, a surge of loyalty shot through her. Tootsie made what she thought of as his Squish Face at her—scrunching his features, his rubbery black lips stretching back to show his little yellow teeth and red-black marbled gums—and his entire body shivered with joy-like intensity. The dog had become fiercely attached to Jackie. Without explanation, she leashed him and stood, worried that she might cry. She didn't want to make a scene. She felt Kent and Susan's eyes on her back as she and Tootsie left. She called over her shoulder, "Gotta go. See you later!" but she sounded falsely reassuring. It was a long walk to the outfield, and she tried not to waddle like Tootsie. To her mortification, she slammed the gate shut behind her.

When she got home, she knew Douglas was pretending not to

hear her enter. Before unhooking Tootsie, she watched Douglas watching a true-life crime show, something about a man who'd murdered his wife. When Douglas was engrossed in television, like now, his mouth opened slightly and it made him look stupid.

Jackie had waited on Douglas many times and flirted, knowing he was a professor at a prestigious private art college. When she'd finally gotten up the nerve to show him some of her drawings, he'd deemed them good and suggested she take his night extension class in art appreciation. She knew these programs were for people who didn't have money or couldn't get in.

Years before, while still in high school, she'd peeled the colorful sticker from this same college off the back window of a parked Lexus and then securely taped it to a mirror in her bedroom, pretending (and aspiring?) to have that magical elixir of wealth, talent, ambition, and confidence; after Douglas had suggested the extension class, she'd scraped the sticker from her mirror in a mixture of pride and shame. But she'd taken his class anyway, and they'd had a quiet affair. Then she'd gotten pregnant and had moved in with him, quitting her restaurant job. She knew now that if they married she'd get a forty-thousand-dollar education for free (she'd checked online: spouses and children), but she tried not to think about this too much.

She unhooked Tootsie, who left for the kitchen, where she heard him lapping from his water bowl, and then she sat next to Douglas. The commercials started and he muted the sound, patting with his other hand for her to sit closer. She inched over so that her thigh touched his and told him about what had happened at the field, surprised at how she couldn't keep the indignation from her voice.

He listened with a glazed expression, and she imagined him thinking, I hope she doesn't want to talk about this. But then he said, "Who cares if they're fucking?"

When she didn't answer he said in his professor voice: "It's at the essence of so many relationships."

"What is?" she asked, already confused.

"The promise of no inconveniences," he said. "No conflicts or confrontations, all the things that create meaningful relationships."

She felt their twenty-two-year age difference most when he lectured her. I'm having a baby with this man, she kept thinking. Jesus H., I'm having a baby with this man.

"Dogs are metaphors," he continued, glancing at the screen to make sure the commercials hadn't ended.

The baby kicked her rib cage.

She often thought about how she'd skipped her birth control pills, and then she'd picture the very moment Douglas had come inside her (doggie-style), breathing into her neck.

"It's not about the dogs," she said. "It's them. This'll mess with our routine. What about Tootsie? He loves the field."

Hearing his name, Tootsie came to her from the kitchen and leaned back in a downward-dog pose, muzzle on his paws and his tail in a slow metronome-wag.

Jackie wasn't sure she loved Douglas. But she'd loved his class.

"Dogs are reflections," he said, unmuting the television now that his show had restarted. "Extensions, conveying their owners' socioeconomic positions."

Douglas didn't love her. He'd told her so. Though he'd also said that he supposed one grew to love one's life partner.

"Am I another mutt," she said, her voice quiet, "for you to save?" She wasn't sure he'd heard her.

Douglas kept his eyes on the screen and muttered, "Mutts are such hardy dogs."

She watched the show with him, knowing she'd have to wait for another commercial break. The man who'd killed his wife had dumped her body—which he'd kept in the trunk of his Nissan Maxima—in a lake during his son's Boy Scout camping expedition, which he'd been supervising as a troop leader.

A serial bachelor, Douglas had had three student affairs before Jackie (that she knew of); but now that a baby was involved, he and his mother (she couldn't get a read on the father) seemed to view the situation as an unexpected bounty, providing him with another kind of life. Along with plying Jackie with prenatal vitamins, his mom had been pressuring Douglas to marry her; both his parents were white-haired blue bloods, and Douglas's hair was going white now, too.

Her own father had died years before in a drug deal gone bad, which had briefly made the papers, and her mom suffered from chronic depression and had been on food stamps for as long as Jackie could remember. Her older sister, a cashier at Rite Aid, still lived with their mother, as Jackie had until she'd moved in with Douglas.

At the commercial break Douglas muted the television. "We treat children similarly," he continued, as if there hadn't been a break in their conversation. "We have to let animals be animals—and dogs, dogs; and children, children. We can't burden them with our troubles and ambitions and expect them to lead healthy lives."

Jackie decided to go back to the baseball field without Tootsie to apologize for her strange and rude behavior. When she arrived, the stadium lights had timed off, diffusing to orange-ending dots.

Kent, on one knee, rubbed Cher's belly, her legs cocked at various angles. Susan and Fozzie had already gone. It somehow seemed like an intensely private moment, and Jackie was about to turn to leave, but then Cher must have caught a whiff of her. The dog rolled, lifted, and barked.

Kent motioned her over, and she walked through the gate to meet them.

They sat at the bench—the stadium lights blacked out now—and she tried to apologize, but he interrupted, saying, "No worries."

They'd not been alone before, and the energy, with the full moon, seemed strange and dreamlike. She was close enough to see a tiny dent and pinprick hole in his left earlobe from having a pierced ear. It surprised her. Chameleon Kent, she said to herself.

Cher, exhausted from all the exercise, huddled at their feet, and when Jackie reached to scratch her ear, the dog didn't budge.

The baby kicked and Jackie leaned back, saying, "Oh!"

Seeming both shy and pleased, Kent said, "Can I feel?"

She set his hand on the side where the baby had kicked, and then the baby thumped again so hard that his fingers lifted. He looked at her and said: "Wow, wow, wowee," and she said, "I know, right?" and he said, "Wow," and they stared at each other and laughed, his teeth and the whites of his eyes glowing.

"I've never felt anything like that before," he said. His eyes had opened wide and he seemed very happy. "What's it like," he asked, "to have a baby growing inside you?"

She thought for a moment. "My body," she said, "like when I sneeze, it doesn't feel like me; and my dreams are crazy. All kinds, in color, too." Douglas didn't want to have sex with her anymore, claiming he didn't want to hurt the baby, but she sometimes orgasmed in her dreams.

Kent said, "It's true what they say about pregnant women."

She felt herself squint in question.

"You're radiant," he said.

Heat rose up her throat and she closed her eyes, feeling his hand go to the back of her neck. A coolness at her front made her open her eyes and she looked down and saw that her sweatshirt had darkened.

"Oh my God," she said, her fingers moving to the dampness at her breast; simultaneously his hand sprang away, as if he'd touched fire.

More liquid came from her.

"What is that?" Kent asked.

"I'm leaking," she said.

"Did I do that?" he asked.

She stood—dizzy—and then she jog-walked in an awkward shuffle to the outfield, making sure not to glance back, even when she shut the gate.

JACKIE HAD EXCHANGED cell numbers with Susan and Kent at the baseball field as a formality. She never expected either of them to call, but Susan did the following morning, asking Jackie to come over, saying she needed to talk in person. Susan pleaded and insisted, and so Jackie agreed.

Susan's house had a For Sale sign on the lawn, deer-shaped bushes, an American flag on a pole, and, attached to the molding of a second-story deck, a USC Trojan-head banner. Jackie parked at the curb and when she walked up the walkway to the front door, a black flat-faced Persian cat watched her from a window.

Susan gave her a tour. Jackie was impressed. It felt like walking through a home in a magazine. She told herself she could dress and live like Susan if she wanted, but she didn't really believe it.

When they circled back to the living room, Fozzie came through a sliding glass door and licked Jackie's hand.

The black cat walked in an arc near them, pretending not to be interested. "That's Smiley," Susan said, noticing Jackie watching the cat. "She's been with me through everything. She's my constant."

Jackie nodded.

Smiley yawned and then gave a hoarse meow.

"A psychic," Susan said, "once told me Smiley's my protector."

This information seemed out of character, and Jackie didn't respond.

"It sounds ridiculous," Susan said. "But who knows?"

They sat on a couch and after Jackie declined something to eat or drink, Susan explained that Kent had called her last night and told her that he and Jackie had had an awkward moment at the field.

Susan grimaced. "I've been so depressed with this divorce; I haven't been thinking clearly. Kent's young and fun, and what we're doing," she asserted, "is nothing serious."

Jackie didn't speak. She had the impression that Susan was implying there'd been a sexual competition between them for Kent.

"I've been insensitive," Susan continued, saying that though she didn't know what Jackie's situation was, she'd like to be more supportive, and that she also hoped to clear up things between the three of them for the sake of their dogs.

Jackie had planned a response on the drive. She said that her OB had told her that she was too far along now to continue taking Tootsie for walks or exercise. "It has nothing to do with you or Kent," she added.

She could tell Susan didn't believe her.

"Your home is amazing," Jackie said to change the subject. "I mean, really, it's fantastic."

Susan seemed pleased. She sighed and said, "We have to sell it anyway."

LATER THAT AFTERNOON Susan called again, and this time Jackie didn't answer. Susan sounded distressed in her voice message, as if she'd been crying, and she asked Jackie to come over. "It's an emergency," she said.

Jackie hadn't made it up the walkway before Susan waved her away, calling out: "I'm sorry. I shouldn't have called. Don't come inside. Please, just leave. You're pregnant! You should go. I mean it." But Jackie kept walking to the front door.

Susan moved aside, and Jackie saw a palm-sized chunk of black fur in the marble entryway, blood streaked along the carpet and walls, and two lamps shattered near the coffee table.

"Kent dropped Cher off for a playdate," Susan's voice said from behind her. "I had a hair appointment, but I decided I could leave the dogs." She'd given them doggie treats, she explained.

They lay on the carpet, Cher's head resting on Fozzie's backside, as she left. "They looked so peaceful," she added.

"Oh God," Jackie said, stepping inside and spotting Smiley's mangled body under the glass of the coffee table.

"They must've done it right away," Susan said, moving forward. She held her elbows across her chest. "The vet says it takes about two hours for the body to get rigid."

Jackie heard a faint whining and scraping sound coming from a hallway closet. "Cher's in there," Susan explained. "There's blood on her, and I found Smiley's fur under her collar. I've left a thousand messages for Kent. Fozzie's clean—no fur or blood on him—but I put him in the bedroom closet. I feel like he contributed. I can't even look at him."

Susan opened a bottle of red wine, and Jackie went to the kitchen for a glass of water. For a moment she contemplated the lone photo of Smiley and Susan in profile with their noses touching, stuck to the refrigerator with a magnet.

Jackie sipped her water while Susan drank a walloping glassful of wine. Then Jackie listened while Susan left another angry voice message for Kent, saying he'd better come get his murdering dog. She'd called Animal Control and they'd be arriving soon to take Cher.

After she hung up, Susan explained that her maid would take care of the mess. She was on her way over. But could Jackie help with Smiley?

Jackie held a white kitchen-sized plastic trash bag while Susan—tear-studded gaze averted—lifted Smiley's body and gently placed it inside.

Jackie cinched the bag around the lumpy weight and set it

on the coffee table. Then she checked on Fozzie in the bedroom closet. His tail thumped twice when he saw her, but he wouldn't come out, huddled in the corner with his head on his paws.

Animal Control came and went, taking both the trash-bag coffin and Cher, who left voluntarily with her tail between her legs.

Before Jackie left, she and Susan sat in wide wicker chairs on the front porch and Susan drank another glass of wine. Monstrous-looking clouds hid the sun and skirted the tops of the mountains, breaking apart and drifting from each other.

"Smiley freezes when she's terrified," Susan said. She took a swallow of wine and added, "She didn't stand a chance."

THE NIGHT BEFORE Jackie gave birth, Susan stopped by. Jackie had forgotten she'd given her Douglas's address. Jackie opened the front door and Tootsie knocked against her legs, trying to get outside. "Sit," she told him, and then, "Down." The trees made a soft shushing noise and a few moths batted against the porch light. She hadn't talked to Susan since Smiley's death. Susan held a present, the wrapping paper decorated with blue and yellow pacifiers. "This is from Kent also," she said. "We met. Cher's in a special dog retraining program," she added. Jackie didn't want to introduce Susan to Douglas. They'd been fighting. But Susan didn't want to come inside. The house had sold, she said. She was moving to Santa Barbara. She handed Jackie the present, and they said their goodbyes.

Jackie went to the bathroom to open the gift in private. She hugged the small, silky blue blanket to her chest, and a heat spread through her at the specter of Kent, along with a flashing involuntary desire; and though she didn't know it yet, the blanket would become her daughter's security object. Jackie would leave Douglas and move from his house, taking their daughter and Tootsie with her. Her daughter would call for Baba, reach and look and cry for Baba. I want Baba! Where's Baba? Babababababa. When Jackie would hand over the blanket, her daughter would wedge it beneath her armpit and stick her forefinger and middle finger in her mouth, sucking, eyes at half-mast and fogging, and relief would spread through Jackie as she watched Baba's narcotic-like influence, a speck of calm and control.

PARKING FAR AWAY

We would meet in the early mornings at the cleaning storage shed: twelve women divided into three groups. Dale kept a list tacked to the bulletin board letting us know our assigned houses. He hired me as an experiment. "You look like a hardworking girl," he said. He looked like Pat Boone. His cheeks were shiny. "Most of the girls never finished high school. None are as young as you, but I think you'll find them very sweet." I'd seen the women milling around the cleaning storage shed, smoking and talking. Most looked beyond childbearing years. "My wife and

I have a Bible study every Wednesday night," he said. "It's not mandatory but is strongly encouraged."

Sun River is a community of vacation homes in Oregon, and our job was to clean four to five a day for the next round of families. We loaded bottles of artificially bright blue and pink cleaning products, buckets, rags, brooms, mops, and vacuum cleaners into three beaten-down hatchbacks, and then unloaded these same items at the end of our shifts. I got tired that first day just loading the car.

"Abby wants to be a writer," Dale said, hand at my shoulder, introducing me to the women. "Be good to her."

The cleaning women treated me with mild curiosity or indifference, asking me innocuous questions and showing me pictures of their kids and grandkids.

Except for Lonnie. Lonnie hated me. The other women warned me: Lonnie's a mean bitch. Ignore her. She's worse when she's drunk, so watch it. Dale keeps her because he has a big heart. If he catches her drunk one more time, she's out.

Lonnie could tell that I came from money and that cleaning houses was a temporary job, a sociological experiment. What Lonnie didn't know was that I was twenty-one, newly sober, recently released from a court-appointed recovery home, and prone to distressing panic attacks. I'd made a mess of my life. Like Dale's Bible studies, a job wasn't mandatory but strongly encouraged, just as making my bed, brushing my teeth, attending twelve-step meetings, and staying away from men were also strongly encouraged.

Later, as we loaded the cars, I saw the outline of a flask in Lonnie's pocket. "Are you a little writer?" she said. "Are you going to write a story called 'How I Cleaned Toilets'? You little bitch."

MY MOTHER WAS a Francophile, her grief from the recent death of my stepfather transforming into a zealous attachment to all things French, including her French teacher from the local community college, now her live-in boyfriend, a small misogynist who wore ascots and verbally abused her. Enzo also preferred Speedo-like underwear, the faint pattern of stripes visible beneath the thin cloth of his tennis shorts like the lines under the ice at an ice rink.

Enzo drove me to work in the early mornings in his truck. We wouldn't speak and I'd watch out the truck window as the dark trees passed. I got rides home from the ladies, but I'd have them drop me off down the block. After their cars disappeared, I'd walk the rest of the way to my mom's big house.

The night after my initial day cleaning houses, I sat across from my visiting grandparents at a restaurant. They were staying in Sun River. Grandma ordered beer, Grandpa his perpetual martini. Behind them against a mirrored backdrop, a wall of liquor bottles shimmered, amber to dark. Half my head went numb, my vision fuzzy.

Grandma's eyelashes fluttered. She was becoming slightly incomprehensible; Grandpa cruel.

"I know why you're cleaning houses," he said. "So you won't end up like her." He beckoned with his martini-hand toward Mom, who held a napkin to her mouth. "You'll end up like her anyways."

"Well," Grandma slurred, "I always believe in leaving a nice tip for the cleaning ladies in an envelope."

IT SEEMED THE rest of the world was getting high while I tried to stay sober. Mom had bought two golden Labrador retrievers, Claudo and Beauregard, to match her house. The dogs wore collars with a square band. If they tried to exit her property, an electrical fence shocked them.

I came home from work late one afternoon to find that Claudo had (once again) sought out the electrical current, positioning himself to be continually shocked. He got high from it, a problem that happened rarely, according to the fence makers. I dragged him away, his tongue hanging.

It was quiet when I opened the front door. Swaths of brightly colored French fabrics lay across the couch and floor. I walked upstairs to my bedroom, the door open. Enzo and Mom were on my bed. I made a cough noise. They stopped kissing and broke apart, Mom buttoning her top. There was an open bottle of Jack Daniel's on the dresser.

Instead of waiting for them to leave, I walked down the hallway.

Mom and Enzo had chosen my bedroom because Hank, a local woodworker, was in their bedroom, installing a mahogany entertainment center.

"Hank's in recovery, too," Mom had informed me earlier, as if it were a hobby. "From heroin."

Hank believed in a liberal methadone recovery system. "Want some?" he asked now, wiping his hands on his pockets, after describing methadone's more admirable side effects.

Hank's bulldog approached me. The dog had a snaggle-toothed underbite and his large genitals hung in a black mass at his backside, his tail a frenetically wagging stub. I tried to hide my shock, feigning casualness as I leaned over to pet his head, but Hank said, "I know, darlin'. Don't worry. He's got giant balls."

I'd been encouraged to stay away from men, but I decided Hank was okay since we shared recovery. I was attracted to him: he rolled his own cigarettes, he had callused hands, he wore frayed Levi's and flannel shirts, and he liked to talk dirty.

My attraction waned three nights later, when his wife called, informing me that not only was Hank betrothed with three children—ages seven to two—but he was also in recovery for sex addiction.

"He was doing just fine until you came along," she said.

LONNIE GAVE ME bathroom duty. The worst part was cleaning pubic hairs. Everywhere: dark curls along the base of walls, various-shaded curlicues on toilet rims, wisps along the cracks in the bathroom tiles, and the inevitable hairy masses in the shower drains. I couldn't control my gag reflex when cleaning pubic hairs.

One afternoon Lonnie was supposed to be making the bed, but she sat on it, the sheets and bedcover a tangled mass on the floor. She tilted a silver flask to her pale lips and her eyes flashed at me. She wiped her palm against her chin slowly and said, "Keep your fucking mouth shut, bitch-whore."

•

THE NEXT AFTERNOON I borrowed Enzo's truck and went to the bookstore. I stayed for hours, perusing books, and I bought Bertrand Russell's *Why I Am Not a Christian*. Dale had been pressuring me to go to his Bible studies.

When I came home, the sun was gone and I could tell that Mom and Enzo had been fighting, the air quiet and hostile.

Enzo wore a bathrobe and stood in front of the open refrigerator door, a slice of light crossing the floor. He sifted, jars clinking, and then he must've heard me, because he shut the door, turned to face me, flicked on a kitchen light, and said something in French. Then he said, "You are a sicko-alcoholic freak, afraid of everything." His eyes glimmered. I could see his chest hairs from a part in his robe. "Boo!" He flashed his hands at me, fingers waggling.

I heard them into the night, yelling and cussing in French.

The next morning he was gone. Mom's eyes were swollen from crying and she wore her blue nightgown. I wanted to make it better, hold her in my arms and rock her, tell her that I loved her, that my grandparents—her parents—were mean, but that I would never be, as if I were the mom. A familiar impulse, as unconscious and natural as my desire to get loaded.

"You'll have to drive yourself to work," she said, handing me the keys to her light blue Mercedes convertible. "I'm done with Enzo for good this time. I promise."

I PARKED MOM'S Mercedes in a strip mall next to a real estate office whose windows were adorned with posters of the houses I cleaned, three blocks away from the cleaning shed, and I walked, to avoid anyone—especially Lonnie—seeing me in the car.

We were on the second house, two more to go, and I was cleaning the toilet with a rag like the ladies had shown me—more effective than a toilet scrubber—when I heard cackling laughter from the bedroom.

Lonnie sat on the bed, her silver flask at her thigh. Her head rolled back and forth as if her neck were made of rubber.

The other two cleaning women decided that one of them would drive me and Lonnie to my car, and that from there I would drive Lonnie home, so that Dale wouldn't fire her. They would finish cleaning for the both of us.

I tried to talk them into letting me stay and clean, but they both laughed and then one of them said, "Oh, honey, you're not very good."

Lonnie and I got dropped off in the parking lot of a Safeway, where I pretended a red Toyota was my car.

"We have to walk," I said to Lonnie, after the cleaning woman's hatchback disappeared around a curve.

Lonnie leaned on me and I half carried her across the inter-section. She wore a shirt with FLORIDA across an image of the state, the F and L faded so that it appeared as ORIDA. We approached the Mercedes and her eyebrows rose.

The tires had been gashed like open mouths. If Lonnie hadn't been with me, I would've suspected her. She let out a noise, "Whoo-hee," not unlike a laugh, but also surprised and serious.

I opened her side with the key and she sat. She leaned across the handbrake and opened the driver side for me.

We sat quietly until she said, "Put the top down."

I turned the ignition and pushed the button. The top rose, moaned, and lay back in folds of canvas.

"Shit," Lonnie said, shaking her head, looking at me with pity. "What the hell's wrong with you? Why the fuck you cleaning houses?"

I started crying.

She set her hands on her knees and waited. I couldn't stop— huge weeping gusts, snot flowing, and I wiped with my shirt.

When I finished, I felt tired and surrendered, as if I didn't have to try so hard anymore. Mom would take Enzo back, I knew. It was a matter of time. But I felt ready.

"Why don't you go?" Lonnie asked finally. She was talking about Dale's Bible studies, but when I didn't answer, she said, "I heard them saying how you and me are the only ones who won't go." She smelled like vodka. I thought about how I drank vodka because I thought people couldn't smell it. Also I loved it.

"Well?" she asked.

"I want to stand on my own feet and look at the world, its beauty and ugliness," I said, badly paraphrasing Bertrand Russell, "and not be so afraid."

She nodded. "You know," she said, looking out toward the trees, "I'm drunk, but even if I wasn't, this is funny."

LONNIE AND I sat in the tow truck with the truck driver. Behind us, the Mercedes shook on the carrier. The driver stopped at Lonnie's apartment and she had her keys in her hand, ready to go.

I already knew it would be the last time I'd see her. I wouldn't show up for work the next morning. Dale would leave an angry message on the answering machine, firing me.

The truck throbbed and shook in park. Lonnie opened her door and hopped down—unsteady—putting her hands out to regain her balance.

The driver released the brake and put the truck into gear. He drove slowly, and I turned to see if Lonnie was watching.

She stood squinting at me near a cluster of mailboxes with her arms crossed in front of her chest, and then she cracked an uncomfortable smile. I wasn't sure it was a smile, and I leaned out the open window to get a better perspective. I saw that it was and that the smile was directed at me, and my heart broke into a thousand shards of sunlight. Then she turned and walked in a zigzag pattern to her door.

WE KNOW THINGS

That summer Gwen imagined confessing. *Mom,* she'd say. *It was my fault. I stole your boyfriend.* But how could she explain? She hadn't even been drunk or high. While her mom was in the bathroom, Sean had paused the DVD (*Unforgiven,* one of his all-time favorites) and his hand went to Gwen. She'd probably given him a look, encouraged him. Sean had leaned forward, kissing Gwen, the living room dark except for the light from the Samsung logo ping-ponging on the television screen. He tasted familiar, safe. In her memory, she pulled away first. But really she wasn't so sure.

What did it matter with the tsunami of sex that followed? Sixteen times, not including the blow jobs.

Her mom had met Sean at her culinary arts class; they'd been dating about a week. She'd told Gwen that she had high hopes and really liked him. He owned two tanning salons, a tire store, and a beachfront home, all in or near Hermosa Beach. The culinary arts class, he'd said, was meant to broaden his scope.

One night after Sean had said that they should end things, Gwen had slipped his Patek Philippe in her purse—denied it whenever he asked—and now she kept the watch in her Toyota Corolla's glove compartment beneath her driver's registration. On eBay, it was worth $4,600.

When Sean had moved to San Diego to be closer to his ex's, where his son lived, Gwen had felt some relief. He'd texted Gwen three sad-faced emoticons and then changed his phone number. But not long after, she'd received three phone calls from a blocked number. The person left heavy-breathing messages lasting a few seconds each, a modulated Darth Vader voice saying: "Where's the watch?" and then, "Hey, slut," and finally, "Sexy whore." She wanted it to be Sean but knew it was probably Zach, Sean's thirteen-year-old son. She'd seen a photograph: brown hair brushed forward in a young Justin Bieber fashion, a determined and sorrowful expression. Tall and thin, reminding her of a puppy not grown into its body, his forearm marked with pen: a peace sign and a star and a flower. He'd probably read the texts between her and his dad before his dad had changed his cell phone number.

Even now after all that had happened, Gwen had trouble moderating that energy, and so she avoided men. Not that her mother was an example: three failed marriages, two affairs, numerous boyfriends.

That summer Gwen avoided her mother. Two weeks had passed since the phone messages. Her dorm at Pomona College felt like a ghost town, and her roommate, a psychology major, had left to backpack Spain. Before leaving, she'd helped Gwen get a job at New Promises, an eating disorder treatment center, where Gwen now worked three days a week. The heat was ugly, mean, smog-filled—even the bushes and grass seemed wilted and bitter.

New Promises, housed in a colonial-style home on a quiet residential street in Claremont, had six bedrooms, four bathrooms, a centrally located kitchen and dining room, meeting rooms, and an entertainment center with a pool table. Despite its homelike atmosphere, institutional touches abounded: sign-in folders, locks at the cabinets and refrigerator, an antiseptic smell. Gwen was sensible and a good worker, and Lauren, the center's manager, appreciated her. Lauren suffered from lupus, which gave her a bloat around her neck and a bulging in her eyes. She was reconnecting with an adult daughter she'd given up for adoption, so an excitement surrounded her. Their office had files with medical records and two computers dotted with yellow Post-its.

The residents (they weren't called "patients") moved through the house like ghosts: fragile, dazed, and medicated bulimics and anorexics, kept on a tight schedule: waking at six; busy throughout the day with group therapy, twelve-step meetings, doctor appointments, psychologist and psychiatrist appointments, nutritionist appointments, mealtimes, art therapy, yoga and meditation, physical rehabilitation, movies and games and social time; lights off at nine.

The youngest, a sixteen-year-old, wore thick overalls on her skeletal frame, her eyes dark and deep, a harrowing sadness. The oldest, sixty-two, had breast implants, a Botox-dead face, and a machine strapped to her chest to monitor her weak heart. She purged and smuggled in laxatives and had to be closely watched, and there was a perpetually fresh wormlike wound on the back of her right hand, created by the recurring drag of her front teeth as she stuck her fingers down her throat. She wore pink Juicy Couture sweatpants with Ugg boots and smelled of Michael Kors eau de parfum, and once she told Gwen, "It's not like I want to be a fuckup."

Gwen wasn't included in group therapy or twelve-step meetings because she didn't identify and had no qualifications. She heard crying, laughter, handclapping. She helped with paperwork, intake calls, menu planning. If she noticed a resident occupying a bathroom for more than two minutes, she gave a backhanded rap at the door with her knuckles (the lockless doors kept two inches open) and called, "Time's up."

Nadie came to New Promises to teach a journal-writing course, and Lauren decided that Gwen should help. As an English lit major, Lauren said, Gwen might benefit. Gwen set up the room with folding chairs in a circle. Nadie lit a hunk of sage with a lighter, both pulled from a woven satchel. She looked to be in her fifties. She waved the sage, walking slowly around the room, letting it smoke. A strict vegan, she'd brought a sack lunch with raw greens and a thermos of soup. Her grayish-brown hair was in a loose ponytail. She never smiled. Tall and imposing, she had a forthright quality and wore jeans and a faded denim jacket, no makeup or jewelry. Nadie was the kind of person, Gwen decided, she would normally avoid: easily offended; humorless; an aura of great past suffering, though she'd probably been beautiful when she was young, with her full mouth, high cheekbones, and something raw and sad about her eyes, a deep brown flecked with green.

The course wasn't mandatory, but seven residents showed with their journals and pens. Nadie spoke about stream of consciousness, the power of words, the giving over of secrets, the discovery of emotions. The journal as a tool to spiritual well-being.

Gwen loved books but had no interest in writing or telling her own story; she came up with just three sentences. The others soon raised their hands, eager to share. A depressed bulimic with an addiction to painkillers wrote about her love for her childhood dog, who'd been hit and killed by a car. Tissues were passed. Another read about her parents' divorce, and how she and her brother were forced to testify against their father, a compulsive gambler and womanizer. More tissues. Another read about how she used to think she was straight. Then bi. Then a lesbian. Now she was leaning toward bi again.

Gwen didn't know what to make of what Nadie read. As a teenager, Nadie had worked at a restaurant. An old white-bearded judge would come in for coffee and pie. Shy and hating attention, Nadie wore large shirts to hide her breasts. Men often commented on her long hair, so she cut it short. The judge told her he liked her haircut and started calling her Duck. Her co-workers and boss and some of the other customers also called her Duck. Months passed and she got used to the nickname. Then one afternoon the judge explained how with her short hair she reminded him of one particular duck. He sat at a bench in the park near a pond and fed the ducks breadcrumbs. This duck, he said, had fewer feathers at the back of her neck, because the males liked her best, mounting her, steadying themselves with their beaks. Eventually Nadie quit her job and let her hair grow. "But to this day," she said, "I'm Duck."

Gwen didn't want to be the only one not to participate, so she read her three sentences, changing the words "my mom" to "someone": *I have a secret that I'll have to keep my whole life. I know it will hurt someone very bad. And that's probably why I did what I did in the first place, which makes me very sad.* The room was quiet, unsure, let down because she hadn't exposed much. After a pause, Nadie spoke, saying that when she was a child, she found out that her parents had been keeping secrets. Her childhood, she decided, had been a lie. "I didn't know who I was anymore," she said. But then she realized that everyone kept secrets and lied, and she let this revelation enrich and complicate her life.

After Nadie left, Gwen folded the chairs and stacked them against the wall, and then she joined Lauren in their office. Gwen asked about Nadie. "She's too intense," Lauren said. Lauren couldn't remember whether Nadie had been a drug addict or an incest survivor or both or none. "In the eighties," she continued, "she was a prostitute, and then she met this Chinese guy. Her sugar daddy, but it was more involved. He was murdered, I think." She paused, trying to remember. "Chinese mafia or something. After that she went back to college, got a bunch of degrees. She volunteers; I don't say no."

THREE DAYS LATER, Gwen stood two people behind Nadie at the Target near her dorm. The man in front of her leaned on a cane, and the woman in front of him had a mop. In her plastic basket, Gwen had a two-pack of lightbulbs, bottled water, and Lays potato chips. Nadie wore leggings with hiking boots and the faded denim jacket. Expressionless, she watched the prices on the screen while the cashier ran her items over the scanner: laundry detergent, hand towels, two bras, ChapStick.

Gwen decided to stay quiet and avoid her. She would have remained undetected, but then the man with the cane coughed and Nadie looked back with a flicker of recognition, and then a serious stare.

Gwen's face heated and she felt her mouth pull into a smile. "Oh, hey," she said, as Nadie approached, stern-faced, carrying her bags, the woven satchel strapped across her chest.

Gwen felt as if she'd been called on something. "I'm sorry," she said. "I meant to say hi, but you were already leaving and I didn't want to bother you." She could see that Nadie didn't believe her. "No, really," she said, and she felt a rush of shame. The tag on one of the bra straps showed through the plastic of Nadie's bag.

"Don't be upset," Nadie said. "I'm not mad. I just look like this."

A noise of relief came from Gwen. The man with the cane smiled at her and then hobbled away. The cashier rang up her items and she paid by swiping her card. She walked with Nadie to the parking lot. It was already dark, the sky streaked with gold and lavender, and the parking lot lights came on with a hissing noise. When they got to her car, to be polite, she asked Nadie whether she needed a ride, believing that Nadie would say no. But she said yes, since she'd probably missed her bus.

Gwen apologized for the mess inside her car. "I keep telling myself I'll clean it, but then I don't," she said. Nadie didn't say anything, fiddling with the car seat, arranging it to a more up-right position.

The drive was quiet except for Nadie's directions, and at a street of similar nondescript apartment complexes, Nadie said, "Stop here. There's no point going farther."

Gwen pulled to the curb, and with the car running, Nadie reached for her bags and then opened the car door.

Without knowing why, before Nadie had fully exited, Gwen said to Nadie's back: "I fucked my mom's boyfriend." She was startled by how angry her voice sounded. Before Nadie could speak, Gwen reached and tugged the passenger door shut. She flicked her blinker and then drove away.

THE NEXT THREE days, Gwen didn't have to work. She read novels in her dorm room, lying on an arrangement of pillows and cushions on the floor like a fortress, the sidewall air conditioner on during the day, a fan rattling next to it. At night she opened the window, set the fan next to the window screen, blowing the cooler air inside.

She inhaled the books like drugs, getting up only to use the bathroom, eat, and go to the college library, which had a new self-checkout system, so she didn't have to talk to anyone. She was used to reading for academic purposes, writing critical essays, spitting back what the professors wanted, but her mind wandered now. There was nothing academic. It was more like she breathed herself into the novels.

Monday morning she received a phone message from a blocked number. "How big are your tits?" she heard, feeling the blood rush to her forehead. This time the voice wasn't disguised; she felt sure it was Zach.

When the blocked number called again, she answered: "I know who this is."

"Slut," said the voice.

"Zach," she said, the blood crashing at her skull, "leave me alone. I'm not with your dad anymore, so leave me alone."

There was a long silence, and so she hung up.

Later that day she was answering phones at New Promises when Nadie stopped by. "I've been thinking about you," Nadie said, "about what happened." Gwen wondered if Nadie meant what had happened when she'd driven her home or what she'd told her had happened with her mom's boyfriend or both. "I came to take you to dinner. But you'll have to drive. I took the bus."

They ate a silent meal at a Vietnamese restaurant, chicken pho for Gwen and a vegan tofu version for Nadie, who was a regular, with fizzy lemonades. Gwen's pho smelled like a Christmas tree, and she wound the noodles with her chopsticks, leaning her face over the steaming bowl. Nadie's composure made their silence easy and comfortable, and the food and drink satisfied her.

Afterward they went to Nadie's apartment for dessert. The building itself was generic, but her apartment was filled with plants, colorful wall hangings, woven rugs, a thick blanket on the back of the couch, a mantel with stones, twigs, feathers, and photographs of her nieces and nephews, who lived in Arizona. Nadie visited and sent money. She'd never had kids. "I couldn't stand the thought of bringing children into the world," she said, "to watch them suffer."

Gwen saw no evidence of a television, computer, telephone, or radio. She sat on the couch, and Nadie opened windows and turned on a ceiling fan, which made a light click-noise from a clanking chain. The kitchen was visible from the living room, and Gwen watched Nadie slicing ginger root for their tea.

Nadie brought the tea and a plate of peanut butter cookies studded with raisins. "No eggs or dairy," she said, setting them on the coffee table. She sat on the floor, tucking cushions under her hips. Comfortable, she looked at Gwen and said, "You don't want to talk, fine. You're angry," and then she told Gwen that when she was ten, her best friend lived next door, John Sullivan. They played together, biked together. Her own parents drank and fought, there was infidelity, but John's home life was more horrific. His mother disappeared for days, and while she was gone, Nadie and John created a tent from the sheet on her bed: touched and kissed and more. Then his mother shot her boyfriend, puncturing his lung, and he died after six days in the hospital. His mother went to jail, and John got sent to his aunt's in Oregon. Nadie and John wrote each other for a long time. Then they lost touch. When she was seventeen, she found out that John had fallen from a cliff. Everyone called it an accident, said that he'd slipped, but she knew. He took a part of her with him, and that next year she went "a little crazy." She heard his voice on the radio, telling her to kill herself. Same for the TV. Drugs and alcohol helped. She ran away, worked at a dance hall. Men paid to press against her, sway her in the dark, buy her drinks. Other things happened, but by then she didn't care. Then a man she called Chi helped her. He wanted her to only be with him, so she was. He wore dark suits and had smooth skin. Like a father, he encouraged her to get her GED. He was involved with criminals, and then he was murdered execution-style, a bullet to the back of his head. Afraid of slipping back to that place where she'd gone when John had died, she stayed clear of all radios and televisions, and she still did. Chi left her money in a savings account. She started college, immersed herself, knowing that he'd approve. When she got her diploma, she was as proud as she'd ever been, and now she had a master's and a PhD, too. She worked part-time at a women's shelter and at an abortion clinic. She didn't need that much money to live. Consumer culture was a sham. "For years, I tried to remember every detail about John, and then Chi. I wore their clothes, only listened to music that they liked. I couldn't separate what had happened with what I remembered, and then with what I imagined. Even now it's changing, because I'm telling you about them."

THEY WENT TO the Vietnamese restaurant the following Tuesday. Nadie took the bus to New Promises, and then Gwen drove. They split the check. After dinner, they went to Nadie's apartment for ginger tea and dessert. They went the Tuesday after that as well, and that evening, sharing a slice of flourless, eggless, dairy-less chocolate cake, Gwen explained what had happened between her and Sean. How it had all started with that kiss when her mom had been in the bathroom.

She and Nadie sat close on the couch, two forks, one plate. Nadie had a crumb on her cheek, and Gwen brushed it off without thinking. She'd deliberated over what had happened so many times that speaking had a redundant feel. But let loose, her secret softened. "When Mom came out of the bathroom," she said, "Sean and I had already moved apart. Mom smiled, noticing the charge in the air. The thing is, I felt powerful. Sick too. Nauseated. But I'd never felt that strong."

Nadie took a slow bite from her fork and then set her fork on the plate. Neither of them spoke for what seemed a long time, and then Nadie said, "Don't tell your mom." She paused, and then added, "She already knows."

Gwen shook her head. "No, no way."

"We know things," Nadie said.

A few minutes passed, and then Gwen told her about the phone messages and Zach and the Patek Philippe in her glove compartment.

"Zach's confused," Nadie said. "Angry at his dad, wants to protect his mom. Hormones," she added, and then, "The watch is a no-brainer." She stood and took their dishes to the kitchen.

Gwen stretched her legs and leaned her head against a cushion. A no-brainer. She had the feeling this would be her last meal with Nadie, and she closed her eyes, and then imagined mailing the watch, care of Sean, to his tanning salon. Packing the watch with bubble wrap and taping the box. But she knew she wouldn't do it.

A FEW DAYS later, Gwen was going over the weekly menu when Lauren came through the office door, looking concerned. "There's this kid outside," she said. "I told him to leave, but he ignored me."

Gwen peeked through the blinds at the window and saw a boy sitting on the curb. Lauren was protective of the women's privacy, so Gwen told her that she'd get rid of him.

It was a bright day, clear and hot, but the boy wore dark jeans and a hooded sweatshirt pulled over his head. He held an iPhone, the white trail of his earbuds leading to it from his hood, shoulders hunched, and his white Nikes contrasted against his dark clothes and seemed enormous, as if his feet belonged to someone else.

When he looked up—a patch of acne on his chin, his mouth open—she recognized Zach.

Zach pulled the earbuds off, and she said, "How'd you get here? How'd you know where I work?"

He shrugged, closing his mouth.

"What do you want?" she asked.

He hung his head and didn't respond. There was something pitiful about him, weak and unformed, and she found herself angry and sorry for him.

The women had free time before group, and two of them wandered outdoors, staring at the sky and listening to the birds. Three others did tai chi in the shade by the side of the house, their movements slow and graceful, like praying mantises.

"Come on," she said, and he stood and followed her to her car, his hands shoved in his pockets. He was taller than she was, and this surprised her.

She opened the car door, retrieved the Patek Philippe from her glove compartment. It felt weighty in her hand. She didn't want to return it to Sean, so giving it to Zach seemed like the best option.

She handed Zach the watch, and he shoved it in his pocket without looking at it. He needed a ride to his friend's in Hermosa Beach. She said she'd take him, and Lauren had no objection to her leaving early, as long as that included removing Zach from New Promises.

Gwen cracked the windows of her Corolla, and as she drove, she told Zach that by the time she was his age, her mom had married her third husband. A space in her chest opened as she spoke and her anger washed away. "I remember when I met my new stepdad's adult kids," she said. "I could tell that they hated my mom, and me by extension. My mom had split up their dad's marriage with their mom, so can you blame them? They had us over for dinner—there were, like, four of them. They faked niceness, extra polite and mean, except for Duncan, his youngest, the fuckup, a janitor or something, I can't remember, the others all on their way to becoming lawyers and doctors. Duncan rolled his eyes a few times at me, to let me know that I wasn't alone."

She felt Zach listening, but he gave no responsive encouragement, his jaw clenched and his big hands at his knees.

"I started to feel really sick," she continued. "I mean, really bad, like I might pass out, and Duncan could tell something was wrong, so he got me outside and we went for a walk and he talked about normal things, like how he'd hated high school, and how he had this fish tank, stuff like that, until I felt all the way better. He smoked Benson & Hedges and was very fat. A few years later—Mom already divorced again—we got a phone call. Duncan had drowned in a swimming pool, drunk and scuba diving. I cried and cried. Mom said, 'You met him once. You didn't even know the man,' but she was wrong."

Gwen was surprised by her talkativeness. Zach remained silent and brooding. She thought of Nadie talking to her, and the anorexics and bulimics ("It's not like I want to be a fuckup"), and her mom, and all the other sad stories. For the first time, she felt strengthened by a connective sadness. She wanted to explain to Zach, push him in another direction, but even before he pressed the button to make his window go down, she had a feeling that he would toss the

Patek Philippe, and that together they would watch it flash, roll, and jump, disappearing in the ivy at the side of the freeway.

"Shit," he said, hands covering his face. He groaned. "Fuck, fuck. Why'd I do that? Oh, fuck. I didn't mean to."

She pulled the car over, and as the trucks and cars sped past, the Corolla shook. "It's okay," she said. "Stay here."

She looked, the ivy dense, stepping over broken glass, a dented chocolate-milk carton, empty cigarette packages, a headless and naked Barbie. Her shirt clung to her with sweat. She wanted to be alone in her air-conditioned dorm with her pillows and books. She glanced over her shoulder to Zach, who'd gotten out of the car with its hazard lights blinking, his face pale and alarmed. He said something, his hair flapping in the wind, but she could only hear the traffic. He started to walk to her, and she waved him away, but he wouldn't stop.

Zach searched the outer edge, and she the middle, and they circled their way around each other. At least five minutes passed, and then a gleam in the dirt caught her attention. She hurried, and when she lifted the watch for Zach to see, a relieved weariness spread through her. Scratched and damaged, the gold-link band broken.

Zach came to her and they embraced, his chest heaving. A honking cement truck passed, causing them to jump from each other, startled. The driver, perhaps mistaking their hug as erotic, continued to honk, the noise shrinking as the truck moved away.

She handed Zach the watch, and he fingered it before slipping it in his pocket. "He's back with my mom," he said. "He's already got another girlfriend. Mom doesn't know."

She disliked that he'd told her, feeling both hurt and surprised.

She wanted to say, You're quite a detective, but instead she started walking to the car. He was behind her, following, when he asked, "What do I do now?" The sun struck blinding glints off the Corolla's back windshield and she shaded her eyes.

He wasn't talking about the watch, but she pretended not to understand. "Sell it on eBay," she said, not looking at him. "Keep the money. I don't know. Give it to your dad. Get rid of it. Throw it back in the ivy."

He slumped in the passenger seat, and she sat behind the wheel, turning the key in its ignition. "I don't know," she said, looking at the dashboard. She wanted to tell him that she'd had no business being with his dad, but instead she said: "I'm sorry. Shit, shit. I really am."

They drove in silence after that, and when they arrived at his friend's, he thanked her. She said that it was nothing and he smiled.

"What do you think you'll do with it?" she asked.

"Don't know," he said, his hand at the door handle, and then he left.

But he'd already decided, because weeks later while finally cleaning her car, she found the Patek Philippe deeply wedged in the crease of her passenger seat.

Not long after, she saw Nadie sitting alone at a bus stop, wearing her hiking boots and leggings and faded denim jacket, the woven satchel at her side. Appreciation spread through her as she slowed her Corolla and rolled down her window. She wondered whether to pull over or call out a greeting, but when she neared the curb, Nadie looked self-contained and expressionless, and so she accelerated and drove on.

FLEDGLINGS

I met Eric first. We were waiting for our free counseling. The psychology grad students got experience, and we poor undergraduates got help. That was the idea anyhow. It was one of those bright, hot, and calm days, but the waiting room had a dank and gloomy feel and smelled of talcum. He was so handsome it made me uncomfortable. A fountain with a spinning rose quartz ball trickled next to a fish tank with a bubbling pirate ship. I pretended to flip through a magazine, every now and then taking him in with quick glances. He was older than I was, which was surprising, as I was an older student in my late twenties. He wore black sneakers and an olive-green

THE SECRET HABIT OF SORROW

T-shirt with YAMAHA written across it in faded lettering. His hair was thick and cut short and had prematurely silvered. "We should leave," he said, his voice stiff and deep, awkward. I would get used to it, though, so incongruent with the tenderness and intimacy he'd share. Sometimes he'd speak in a quickening staccato, with that same rigidness, his words trying to keep up with his thoughts. "They don't know what they're doing anyway. Last session, my counselor started crying."

I nodded. "Mine gasped," I said, "when I told her about my family."

He laughed appreciatively. "You can't beat the price," he said. "Mine's keen," he added, tapping at his temple, "on figuring me out."

"She likes you," I suggested.

"Then she's headed for the iceberg," he said. "I'm like that shopping cart with a purposefully wobbly wheel. A choice to throw people off."

I suggested he get a heterosexual male counselor or a lesbian one.

"Why?" he asked.

"You're too handsome," I said, deciding to get that out of the way.

"Thanks," he said. "Maybe I should start wearing a werewolf mask." He smiled and his face went childlike. I never got used to how his face could change, becoming open, young, joyful, and faultless in a flash. Then his age returned and he said, "You're good-looking, too."

"I'm not super ugly," I conceded.

"Depression?" he asked.

"Constant anguish," I said. "Doom in the bones. I'm off antis."

"I got off last year, too. Prozac. A brief stint with Zoloft."

"I have to be careful," I said. "Depression becomes physical with me—like in my body."

He nodded. "I hate those ads," he said, "where the woman's wincing in physical pain until after the drugs, then she's laughing and swinging her groceries." He paused and then changed the subject: "You ever date dumb people? It's the worst."

"I dated a dumb trust-funder named Edmond," I said. In those years I was only sexually active with men who couldn't challenge me. The sex was bland, but it felt safer.

"The worst is dumb with attitude," he went on. "Sassy dumb. They're the type," he said, looking at the fish tank, "who tap on the glass and go, 'Hey there, fishy, fish.' God, I hate that. Stay away from glass-tappers."

WE DECIDED TO be roommates and found an apartment near our campus in Riverside. The apartment was next to a popular Thrifty's where we'd buy our ice cream, its parking lot full, and a HoneyBaked Ham store. That first day, I remember Eric sat on the couch and drew his sweatshirt up over his head. Then he folded it neatly in the bright light and set it next to him, like an old man would. He drank his coffee and espresso in the mornings like booze. Shots upon waking, while squinting and leaning against the refrigerator. This was in 1992, when earthquakes frequently rattled the region. I could feel the earth rumbling beneath my feet in aftershocks when I walked to my classes. We liked being far from Los Angeles, in a place that seemed more like a desert, but not too far. The main street was loaded with prostitutes, and crack had taken over, though it would soon switch to crystal meth.

We were both sober, determined to revive our lives, and this meant an education; we'd fucked up before, getting kicked out of colleges, ruining opportunities, nearly dying. Now was different. My grandmother—also an alcoholic but more hardy than me, drinking until the very end (the first time I drank, I ended up hospitalized and on a ventilator)—had died and left me money. I knew she'd want me to use it to graduate from college. He afforded rent and tuition via his work as an extra on television shows, commercials, and movies—his specialties: doctors, lawyers, politicians, and policemen. His grandfather and great-grandfather had both been police chiefs back east, while other relatives had been bootleggers. Criminals on one side, the law on the other. Same thing, really. But he used his looks and played the authorities, not the criminals. He wasn't a good actor, because of his stiff voice and demeanor, but he could stand and look the part and say a line or two, and he had steady work. He introduced me to his favorite deceased actors: Theda Bara, Harold Lloyd, Mabel Normand, Claude Rains, and Ralph Waite.

Eric took the room with the largest closet, since he had an extensive wardrobe: doctor lab coats, police boots, formal wear, a '70s tux, a tan-colored jalabiya, a beekeeping outfit, snowshoes, swim fins, porkpie hats, moccasins, oxfords. He kept a photograph of his younger brother—bearded, long-haired, extensively tattooed—on the bedstand. "People think," he said, "by the way we look, that my brother's the crazy one. But we fooled them: he's a lawyer, I'm the drunk." He had three sisters and two brothers, spread across the states. "My immediate family," he said, "is tight. We don't talk much, but it doesn't matter. Like soldiers who've weathered a war." His dad had been violent and had died of alcoholism. Being an extra was like an extension of his childhood. "Ever since I was small," he said, "I dressed up in funny outfits to humor my depressed, battered, bleeding, crying mother."

The mountains loomed behind our complex, and we liked being surrounded by them, especially at night, a deep darkness shadowing the dark sky. There was a lit-up cross on the crest of one. Sometimes we hiked a mountain trail at night to its peak, where, breathing the air, we watched the lights shimmering below in the darkened landscape, like a multicolored upside-down constellation. Our next-door neighbors were loud partyers who belonged to a sorority and watched scary movies—the hyped-up music and screams filtered through the thin walls. At the center of the complex was a pool lit by underwater lights so that it glowed like a jewel. At the bottom, kids' toys—dolls, pool rings, plastic animals—wavered as if stranded in an imaginary current.

THEN I MET Olive. I saw her walking on campus with a determined brisk step, a halo of gloom surrounding her. Old enough to be a professor, tall, willowy, head down as if braced against a strong wind, she wore a bulky dark blue corduroy jacket with a woolen collar that looked like clustered cotton balls, her hands pocketed. No matter the heat, she wore it. Later I found out it belonged to her older half brother, who'd committed suicide on his thirty-seventh birthday. They'd fooled around as kids, playing doctor and such, until she'd gotten old enough to say no more.

She didn't tell me this until she knew and trusted me. But the first time I met her was during my human sexuality class, which she'd crashed that morning, curious about our guest speaker, who had AIDS. "I'll be dead by next year," he said into a microphone. We stood against the wall in the back of the auditorium—it was a packed class—and her arm accidentally pressed against mine. "Sorry," she said, moving over. Her gaze was steady and serious and she seemed to assess me. Finally she said, "I've seen you around. Are you available for lunch?"

We went to the cafeteria. Her eyes, gray-colored and lit with a bemused sadness, were slightly Asiatic—her Hungarian blood, she claimed. She dipped her spoon into a swirled pile of coconut and mango frozen yogurt, but she barely ate. I had a grilled cheese sandwich and French fries. She asked for my pickle and I gave it to her. She set it on a white paper napkin and didn't eat it, perhaps forgetting. "I'm missing my economics class," she said. "Fuck Marx. He didn't see how far down people are willing to go. I touched your arm," she continued, "and thought to myself: 'Self, you can reach out to this woman, who seems beguiling yet troubled, and ask her to lunch, or you can forgo that and dedicate yourself to the far more tempting yet arduous task of isolation.'"

Olive Nelson was named, she claimed, by her mentally ill mother, who drank martinis with olives and worshipped her sons but hated Olive. "No, really," she said, noticing my disbelief. "She hated me." When I told her that my philandering stepfather had died from a stroke the year before, after my mother had neglected to take him to the hospital, she said, "Don't worry, my mom might've murdered someone, too." In private Olive was emotive and expressive. In public I was lucky to get a handshake.

"I'm quite wooden," she admitted. "I'm also quite critical of my gender. But you, Ellie Wilson, I like."

Nearing forty, Olive had already been twice divorced, finally getting her BA, living off spousal support "just barely." She claimed to rent a garage for a room from a friend of a friend, but she wouldn't let me come over, so I never saw her living space. The husbands had left her, the latest a psychoanalyst, accomplished and rich. "People always assume I'm the one who left. I married both times," she added, "because I loved the men's parents. I'm often making sure other people adopt me. Not that I'm needy. I gather influences to fight the forces that raised me."

She'd say, "Goodbye for now," when she left, emphasizing the words "for now," like an assertion of hope that we'd have another day.

OLIVE CAME TO the apartment on May 15 to surprise me with a picnic in celebration of Saint Dymphna's feast day. "Who's Saint Dymphna?" Eric asked, helping Olive spread a blanket on our living room carpet.

"Patron saint of the insane," she said cheerily.

She handed him a pamphlet on Saint Dymphna from the picnic basket, and he read for a few silent moments, then commented: "Also the patron saint of victims of incest. Looks like the earliest recorded history of victim blaming and an inspiration for Woody Allen. A tough day to celebrate. Dad cutting off her head." He sighed, and then added: "Those Irish—I'm one, so I can say this—are fucking tragic."

"It was either a picnic," Olive said, taking off her brother's jacket, "or the Korean spa. But I'm not sure Ellie would've appreciated the experience." She sat on the blanket and smoothed her skirt with a palm. "They put you in a mugwort bath, and everyone's naked except for the ladies in black underwear, who strip off your outer skin and scrub you with hard brushes like you're a dog." She looked up. "Even between your legs," she said in a confidential whisper. "Afterward," she said, "you're swaddled like an infant in a cotton robe."

"Mmhmm," Eric said. It was his sexiest expression, deepthroated and soft, and he didn't employ it often.

She smiled coquettishly and added, "You're quite attractive. No wonder Ellie's been hiding you. You remind me"—she placed her palm on her heart—"of my childhood flame. He lost his arm in a motorcycle accident. Nothing ever happened between us, but he touched my stomach in a pup tent one night."

"I've been lucky," Eric said. "My last motorcycle accident was in Tahoe, tossed forty feet headfirst into a ravine between rocks and trees. Mostly cuts and bruises. Right shoulder rebuilt. Before that, a few car wrecks: back, chest, face, head."

"I get it," she said. "After I survived a fatal illness many years past, I told my husband, now ex, that I realized I find it easier to die than to live." She paused and then added thoughtfully, "I think I scared him."

Eric went to the refrigerator and pulled out what he called his East Coast white Irish potato salad to add to the picnic. "Ultra basic," he said. "Celery, lettuce for effect as a bowl, no eggs."

"My half brother and I," Olive said, "used to picnic as kids. We'd pretend-smoke Grape Vines licorice and read plays and Rilke poems to each other. Voices, faux-foreign accents, the whole shebang. We weren't aware it was pretentious or artsy, just figuring out how to enjoy our neglectful parents' books."

"It's not pretentious," Eric commented, his face flashing child-like, "I don't think, if you're not aware."

She nodded grimly.

"The TV," Eric said, "raised me. I know it's not very California, but I've accepted the TV as my friend. I've tried to give it up, but it's always there when I need it."

We sat on the floor and ate and talked, though mostly I ate and listened and they talked. Outside the sky changed colors until it went from a gray smear to dark blue. When she found out that Eric was sober like me, she said, "A guy 'in the program,' as you call it, took me on a date whose first stop was a hardware store. It did not bode well."

"What happened?" I asked.

"Well, he pulled out lengths of chain and asked a helpful salesperson where the hooks section was. I began to perspire unhappily." She handed me a deviled egg. "I have the trouble," she continued, "of not wanting to embarrass someone by being revolted in advance of what may be happening."

We listened to our neighbors' excited murmuring banter and footsteps as they tottered out their front door. "High heels," Eric commented.

Olive nodded. "New," she said. "Listen. They've not worn them before and are awkward."

After they clip-clopped past our front door, Olive said, "My friend in boarding school lived in the dorm bedroom next to mine with an adjoining door. At night he scratched the door like a giant cat."

We were quiet for a moment and then Eric said, "When things get too good for me, I leave. I've moved so many times."

"I'm a bolter, too," Olive said. "But that's unusual: leaving when things are good."

"Eric starts talking," I said, "about Spain or the Cayman Islands, and I know it's time to be rude or make life more difficult for him, so I do my best."

"Vanishing," Olive said, "is a useful skill. But it can be like ending a poem before the true last line comes into being. Do you need time alone now?" she asked him. "You seem like you might need to take cover."

"No," Eric said with real sadness. "I like you both so much."

Olive put her hands in her hair as if overcome. Then her hands went down and she said, "Wow. We are chatty. I often regret opening the door on the cave after months of darkness. But here I am and somehow we found each other."

"YOU HAVE NO reason," Olive told me a month later at the knife store, "to be jealous."

We'd all three decided to stay in Riverside for the summer. Take classes and be together. Olive wanted to buy matching Opinels, which she claimed to be a good starter knife. Yet Eric had gone for a walk in the park instead. He liked to listen to Judy Collins sing "Both Sides Now" on repeat and pretend he was in the sixties and everything was okay.

"He doesn't want me," Olive said, peering through a glass case at the displayed knives. "I'm ten years older, I live in a garage, and I'm missing teeth."

"You are?"

She pulled the edge of her mouth with her pointer finger, exposing a black gap about three teeth large near her upper molar. She let her mouth go and said, "Imagine tongue-kissing that."

I felt my chest tighten, envisaging the inevitable abandonment. "I'm tired," I said, "of God's dry hands on my ass. But I'll see how it unfolds."

"We're sexual cripples," she said. "Eric, too. I can tell he's been molested. Something happened to you. Intimacy is not our forte."

A pang went through me: Eric had told me about a priest his mother had welcomed into their family. The priest had wooed seven-year-old Eric, letting him drive his Cadillac, as long as he did so naked. He'd also told me about a math teacher/track coach who'd taken him north to Greenwich, ostensibly to do grave rubbings. The man was in jail now.

"There were pedophiles in my and my half brother's life, too," Olive said, as if reading my mind. "It was always hard to let them down, that is, when I managed to preempt things. Sad people."

When I didn't respond she said, "My mom's lover fondled me when I was very young. He was more like a father to me than my dad. When I told my mom, she slapped me. Yet she'd dangled me out in place of herself."

I hesitated. But then I said, "My dad's friend deflowered me, whatever you want to call it. It was brutal. I didn't know how to have sex. My parents left me with him. Big mistake."

"Oh," she said quietly.

"I trusted everyone," I said, "and felt if I countered their desires I'd not be loved."

"Yes," she said.

"Love was the last thing on his mind. I wasn't geared to say no."

"Normal," she said.

"I guess."

"There's a reason," she said, "for statutory."

"No one found out."

"Sadly common," she said.

Shame welled inside me and I said, "I'm sorry. I'm disgusting."

A flicker of empathetic sorrow crossed her face. "When you, me, and Eric are together," she said, "it's like we're lying in sleeping bags looking at the stars and talking. I, too, have a hard time with our bodies entering this equation. You're not alone in this."

A prickly sensation engorged the area behind my nose and eyes, but I managed not to cry.

"Our desires," she continued, "are beautiful and wholesome, like licking a mixing spoon and testing the batter." Her voice went severe: "Don't you dare be ashamed."

A LONGING FOR physical contact thundered inside me after that, drowning out my other thoughts, gathering such force I worried it was visible, like another arm. One night Olive, Eric, and I watched *Fanny and Alexander*, lying on the floor in front of the TV among a stack of pillows and blankets. I got up to make microwave popcorn, watching the bag revolve, expand, and pop in the light of the microwave oven. I wore shorts and a T-shirt, no bra, and I ran my hands lightly over my stomach and breasts. I'd become aware of myself through Olive and Eric's appreciative eyes, and a revelation had dawned that my body possessed a whole tract of unmined and unlimited potential, which I now wanted to explore.

At some point the movie ended and we all fell asleep, Eric in between Olive and me. But then I heard their murmuring, Eric's back to me. "Go to sleep," I told them. Not long after, the murmuring started up again, like water running from the hose outside, and though I wanted to tell them to stop, I didn't. Confused, I fell back asleep. Sometime later I woke. The room was dark, the only light coming from a streetlight outside the window. They were quiet—too quiet.

The following morning, Olive and Eric behaved as if nothing had happened. But I caught a look of rewarded, shared intimacy between them. I felt swollen with sorrow at my exclusion, and I was angry that I'd given them the opportunity.

SOON AFTER, A lot happened quickly. Olive got arrested. We found out that she hadn't been living in a friend of a friend's garage. She'd been staying at a downtown motel. Olive would sometimes hear a prostitute crying in the room next to hers. Anguished sobs. Olive would run into the prostitute's pimp in the hallway and glare at him. But one afternoon, she pulled a knife (her Opinel, as it turned out) and stabbed the pimp in the stomach. The pimp had been hospitalized for internal bleeding. Olive's ex—the psychoanalyst—had bailed her out of jail. She came by the apartment on a Sunday afternoon to say her goodbyes. Her ex waited at the curb behind our complex's iron fence in his chocolate-colored Mercedes, head down, a bespectacled, chubby man.

"Philip," she said, "is quite upset. This is going to cost him, but fortunately he knows the best lawyers." We stood outside by our welcome mat, all of us squinting in the bright sun without sunglasses. She only had a few minutes. Her hands were pocketed in her brother's jacket, and her hair had a swirly bump at the back of her head, like she'd slept on it wet. We could hear kids playing Marco Polo in the pool. The pimp, she said, would live. She'd been expelled from the college. Her ex was letting her stay at his place in Malibu. His new wife had agreed, having always liked Olive.

Caught up in her story of stabbing a pimp, I was not as sad about her leaving as I would be later. I was also excited about having Eric to myself again. Olive must've seen something in my expression, because she went on one of her potent tangents, saying, "What a gas it is that the common use of 'platonic' for nonsexual love comes from Plato's theory of ideal forms that don't exist—can't exist—in earthly life." She looked directly at me, adding, "We are mere shadows. Ha!"

Philip honked his horn and she turned, waved to him, and then faced us, saying, "I was determined as a child not to give up something I really did love about me. I don't know what it is. But our friendship reminds me of this." She smiled. "Maybe," she said, "it's simply being given life."

"Hold on," Eric said, and then he went back inside. He returned with a braided, tweedy-looking thing. "It's a piece of dead cholla cactus," he said, handing it to Olive. "I found it when I went to Joshua Tree."

She was pleased. She said, "My mom used to tell me, 'A woman must never accept anything from a man unless it's a wedding ring.'" She pointed the cholla to the sky. Then she pressed it against her chest, saying: "I shall treasure it."

I tried in vain not to feel jealous. She hugged me and then went on tiptoe to hug Eric, saying, "You are tall. I forget until I see you." They let go and she went down, adding, "Yet you have developed a subtle way of not towering."

Philip honked again, and she started for the car. We watched her cross the cement path to the gate. She opened it, then turned and called, "Goodbye for now," smiling and waving her hand.

THAT NIGHT ERIC and I slept together for the first time. A space opened and something had to happen. We missed her. There was tenderness, grief, and consolation in our sex. The whole time I felt caressed and gently held, my skin humming.

I went on the pill. We got better with time and practice, like we occupied one body, deciding how to pleasure it, nothing off-limits. I enjoyed being physically overpowered and he complied. One night he shivered, saying, "Oh my God, oh my God," and I felt him holding back, so I repeated his words to him, and we gained a rhythm and momentum. We negotiated, everything ripe for exploration, and we had fun. Sometimes he wore his costumes.

When he left a few months later, I knew that our relationship had been good for him as well.

FROM TIME TO time I still spot Eric in commercials, movies, and television shows: the policeman, politician, doctor, or suited man in the background, his beautiful face squinted and sincere. It's like seeing a ghost. Afterward it's impossible to focus on the story line. He wrote me once, whereas I've not heard from Olive, at least not yet, and haven't been able to track her down. He expressed regret for having left me in Riverside, though he gave no indication of wanting to reconnect. *Sometimes,* he wrote, *I feel like a dream walker, like I can't connect to life. But I do my best.* He was grateful for our time in Riverside. It had fundamentally changed him, he claimed. In fact it had kept him alive. *My half-Swedish grandmother,* he wrote, *used to laugh with no sound. Being with her I felt safe. As a kid, I'd watch TV as she slept in the chair next to me. I felt the same with you and Olive.* There was no return address and he has no Internet presence; otherwise, I would tell him what I believe he already knows: My relationship with Olive and Eric propelled me toward the world and to other people, instead of leaving me to burrow further into my wounded self. "You are in me," as Augustine puts it, "deeper than I am in me." Or as Eric wrote: *I can't imagine me without you and Olive. You know how it is. You keep people with you.*

DC

Elaine wouldn't normally get lip, cheek, and eye fillers. She wasn't the type. But it was like—along with her husband, house, and family—she was divorcing herself. Who was she? She'd been the one to discourage friends who talked about getting work done. Dye your hair, sure. Alter your face and body? How could you call yourself a feminist? Have some dignity. Yet a routine dermatologist appointment had turned into thousands of dollars spent with a swipe of her Visa. The needle sliding into her skin had felt painful and strangely reassuring, and she'd craved a stronger violence, something more extreme like surgery. Little bumpy purple dots were emerging along her upper lip line, where the injections had been. She tried not to smile, laugh, or cry like the dermatologist recommended for the first forty-eight hours. One day down, one more to go, and then she could emote.

Elaine had slept coffin-like on her back last night and woken in a panic, unable to recall where she was, the domed smoke detector on the ceiling unfamiliar, her bedside digital clock, the blank walls. When she turned the blinds on the window and saw the yellow-lit Hi-Life Liquor sign from the corner store, it all came back. Now she confined herself inside, not visiting Serena in the conjoining apartment, though it was the weekend and Serena's kids were off sailing somewhere with their dad and his girlfriend. Serena, Elaine knew, would be expecting her. Elaine had gone as far as to kick out the brick that wedged open the automatically locking iron gate dividing their patios, a signal to Serena to leave her alone.

Serena had helped Elaine transition into the Palm Garden Apartments in Costa Mesa: demonstrating how the garage gate remote worked at a certain angle, showing her where the mailboxes were located and how to jiggle the key to open hers, explaining how the garbage cans should be set in a specific spot along the sidewalk pre–trash day or the trash men wouldn't empty them.

"Neighbor!" Serena's voice had sung out that first day, before her face had appeared at the patio. "Welcome to divorce Shangri-La!" Large, golden-brown skinned, and barefoot, she wore sweatpants, a T-shirt, and a Boston Red Sox hat. She opened the gate with a key and then nudged the brick with her foot to keep it open. "You've got the look of the big D," she said.

Elaine was used to insta-intimacy between women but sensed Serena had been betrayed, so she made a decision not to disclose her mistake: the affair. She explained that she and her husband were separated, and that their son, Adam, was a sophomore at Boston University.

"Got him to college first," Serena said. "Way to go, Momma!" Her cheeriness had an edge of hostility and her eyes were vaguely bloodshot. She handed Elaine a tinfoil-wrapped paper plate with three pieces of cassava cake. "Proud Filipina," she told Elaine. "Classic story: supported my ex through med school so that he could leave me for a younger white woman, and the fucker got a nose job, too."

Was she drunk? No, but Elaine came to understand that Serena smoked pot when her kids were with their father, and that she had the predilections of an adolescent boy, like Adam at thirteen. Sans kids, Serena abandoned self-care routines like showering and brushing her teeth, watched sports, played Xbox in bed, smoked pot, fiddled with porn on the Internet, and ate junk food.

The apartments—the first and only complex Elaine had visited—were a sterile fawn color, three levels in a U shape around a pool, theirs on the ground floor facing the street and Hi-Life. They were temporary tenants: Elaine until she figured out what to do (maybe in time her husband would take her back), and Serena until after she and her ex split the money from the sale of their home, now in escrow, so they could buy homes of their own. Usually people were impressed when Elaine told them that she and her husband were professors—he in economics, she in English—but Serena was not. Sometimes when Elaine used the bathroom—as late as two or three in the morning—she could see through a small corner of the mottled-glass window the flickering blue light from Serena's laptop in her bedroom and Serena's shadowy, alert profile, or the quick burst of a lighter flame as Serena lit her glass bong. Serena barely slept! The apartments looked the same from the outside and came with matching brown welcome mats, though Serena had swapped hers for a mat with a cartoon depiction of Lionel Richie that read *Hello . . . is it me you're looking for?*

Serena's kids—the daughter seven, the son nine—stayed with Serena on Monday, Tuesday, and every other Wednesday, and with their father the latter part of the week, weekends tossed back and forth between the two, divided by law. Serena avoided Elaine when her kids stayed with her, becoming an indifferent, industrious, and responsible stranger. The girl had obviously been told she was pretty too many times and thus spoke in an affected baby-doll voice, clinging like a monkey to anyone who gave her attention. The boy had been stung by a bee one afternoon at the pool and had overreacted, scaring Elaine with his screaming; later she saw him crouched and whimpering in a dark stairwell, and when she'd approached to comfort him he'd waved her away.

Serena worked as an office manager at the same hospital where her ex was a surgeon—they'd met as students at Harvard—and Elaine had seen them interact only once. His mouth full of silver from braces, he looked trim, preppy—like a well-groomed WASP. Despite his midlife-crisis upgrades, Elaine had witnessed from her patio—in the silent handoff of their children at the street—Serena's contemptuous glance shoot right through him, leaving him staggered.

Elaine pressed her thumb against the hot, spongy skin near

her upper lip, moving closer to the mirror near her bookcase. The bumps seemed brighter and bigger, and others were forming underneath her eyes. She refused to go online and read about side effects; it would frighten her. Her husband, she imagined, would be napping on his side, his hands cradled between his knees, their dog in her place on the bed. He'd been shocked when she'd told him about her affair. He'd taken the betrayal quietly, but it was a deal breaker. She'd been cavalier and foolish, and he was proud. She longed for the restorative protection of their marriage now that it was gone. Her mother-in-law hadn't seemed surprised and, in fact, had seemed smugly satisfied, while her own father was hurt and embarrassed. Her mother was dead, thank God, coming on five years, though she wished she could talk to her now. Adam's independence had coincided with the affair; when he'd left for college, she'd felt a surge of irrational freedom that had fooled her into thinking it came without consequences. Adam barely called or emailed now. A two-month affair exploding a twenty-three-year marriage. Before this, love had followed an easy and straightforward course. She'd do anything to take the affair back, or at the very least take back telling her husband.

The man she'd had the affair with—she wouldn't think or say his name—would be out somewhere with his girlfriend. She imagined them kissing: he'd run his thumb along his girlfriend's chin the way he used to do with Elaine. How could she have been so stupid? A younger man, he would check out other women— younger also—when they were together. Part of the challenge had been keeping his attention. She'd met him at the gym—such a cliché. By the time she'd realized it was merely physical, she'd already dived into the swamp of sex and delusion. She shivered at the horror, understanding again and again and again how she'd traded so much for nothing.

DC, her friend Hannah would have warned—about the affair, the fillers—had she not died from bone cancer three months after Elaine's mom had passed. They'd been friends since the fifth grade. In high school, a fifteen-year-old girl had been raped and murdered, her body found on the soccer field. Dead Catherine, she and Hannah called her. Catherine had gotten into her perpetrator's car—apparently she barely knew him—and everyone seemed to agree that she should have known better. Dead Catherine became a warning. Like when Hannah wanted to hitchhike. Dead Catherine, Elaine said, and they didn't do it. They shortened the code. Used it for lesser dangers as well. Elaine would be talking to a man at a party, and she'd glance in Hannah's direction. *DC*, Hannah would mouth, and Elaine would walk away from him. The last time Hannah had said "DC" had been when Elaine had said she might try a colonic.

Elaine heard the suction sound of Serena opening her patio door. Serena smoked pot outside, leaving blackened, shriveled matches. A few minutes later a fist thumped against Elaine's own patio door. The curtains were closed, but she knew it was Serena. The brick hadn't stopped her: she'd used her key on the gate.

Elaine called out, "Hey, not feeling hot, just want to be alone," her lips fattened. Through a crack in the curtains, she saw Serena's hand starfish-like against the glass.

"It's an emergency," Serena said. "Open the door."

Elaine wished it were her husband demanding to see her. She moved the curtain and slid the door open.

"Oh, hell no," Serena said at the sight of Elaine's face. Serena wore what she called her magic muumuu. Blue with a V neck and embroidered with whales, flowers, and women hula-dancing.

"Fillers," Elaine said, blood thumping in her lips. "It's getting worse," she said.

"Oh, honey," said Serena, "it's terrible."

Tears sprouted and Elaine swiped them, saying, "I'm not supposed to cry."

Serena went online and researched. She helped ice Elaine's face, but the bruising, swelling, and bumps remained. She called Elaine's dermatologist and left a voice message, though he was out for the weekend.

"If it gets worse," Serena promised, "we'll go to the ER."

Before long, Serena said that she needed Elaine's help, too. "I wasn't lying," she said, sitting at the couch with Elaine. "It's an emergency." As a joke, she explained, she'd messed around on a Trump dating site. She hadn't voted for Trump, FYI. The site was for people who "support our president and want to hook up," and she'd gotten very high and interacted in "a very sexual way" with some "scary men, to mess with their heads," and then had stupidly accepted a couple of date requests and given out her address and this one man was all talk, but this other one, well, he was on his way from Fontana right now and would be here soon and he was not a good man.

Elaine said, "Maybe it'll be okay. Is he cute? Maybe you'll like him. Just because he supports Trump doesn't mean he has to be awful."

Serena slumped into the couch, saying, "It doesn't matter. I didn't use my photo or my name." She peered at Elaine. "Maybe," she said, cheerful but with sarcasm, "Mike—that's the guy coming now—will fall in love with me. He'll have a brother or cousin or friend or something, and I'll introduce you, and then we'll both have men. Too bad," she added, "he's a racist who collects guns."

"You gave him your address?" Elaine said.

Serena met her eyes and said, "He's not a nice man."

A nearby dog's chirpy bark corresponded with the musical chime of Serena's doorbell.

"He's here," Serena whispered.

The man—Mike—pounded his fist at the door and said, "I know you're home, Amber!"

"Amber?" Elaine said.

Serena snorted but looked frightened.

He knocked for a long time. Then after a long pause, the doorbell chimed at Elaine's door. They both stared at each other.

"Hello," Mike said, pounding, "hello, hello, answer!"

Elaine stood and went to the door. Through the peephole she saw him: large, pink-faced, middle-aged, weedy-looking hair, wearing jeans and a muscle T. On one bicep a coiled snake tattoo, on the other a Confederate flag with REBEL written across it. No gun as far as she could tell. Despite everything, he had a slightly effeminate demeanor, his freckled face bunched in a goofy grimace.

"Amber doesn't live here," Elaine said.

"Where is she?" he asked. "Tell her Mike is here."

"No Ambers live here or next door or in these apartments."

"What's your name?" Mike asked.

Elaine paused, trying to think of another name. But she said, "Elaine."

"Hell, Elaine. I drove all the way from Fontana. Can you please open the door?"

Elaine looked over her shoulder at Serena. "When he sees we're not Amber he'll leave," she said.

Serena said, "Maybe, maybe not."

Elaine opened the door and Mike seemed surprised.

"Satisfied?" Elaine said. "Now leave."

His head went back and he squinted, saying: "What happened to your face?"

"Don't worry about it," she said.

He said, "Holy shit," and then with pity, "You should see a doctor."

"Don't worry about it," she repeated.

He stayed in the doorway and then his attention shifted to Serena. He stared for a long minute and she stared back. A growing awareness seemed to dawn between them.

"Cunts," he muttered, before leaving. "Fat, ugly bitches."

Elaine felt stung. Serena appeared grief-stricken. For a long time they sat at the couch and didn't speak. Then Elaine broke the silence, saying, "Why'd you give that man your address? What were you thinking? He has a Confederate flag tattoo!"

"I was drunk and high," Serena said. "Bored and lonely, trying to have fun. I didn't realize I'd given him my address until this morning." She paused and then added, "It's like I do bad things even though I know it's stupid." She gave Elaine a questioning look. "You had an affair," she said. "That's why your husband stays at the house and you're here. I'm not dumb. You're too scared to tell me. Rightly so."

Elaine said nothing, thinking about Hannah and her mom

and how disappointed they would have been. Had they been alive, her fate—her decisions—might've been different. Her face warmed as she flashed on a memory of the man she'd had the affair with staring at her across the gym while doing one-armed push-ups; and then later he'd stared at her the same way while thrusting down on her during sex. She felt an involuntary wetness at the crotch of her underwear.

After a minute or so Serena said, "Whatevs. I'm not mad at you. I was at first. But I'm over it. The things we do that fuck us— maybe they're our own fucked-up way of shouting 'Fuck you' to the world."

Relieved, Elaine nodded in agreement.

"Mike's face," Serena said, shaking her head, "oh my God, when he saw you!"

They laughed and Elaine protested, saying, "Stop, stop! It hurts!" Her face pinched with pain, but the laughter was uncontrollable and continued. She wiped at her eyes, pulling herself together, but then she heard Serena mutter, "Amber," and the laughter started again.

When they were finally done Serena said, "Phew!" Then she said she'd try dating sites again. She wouldn't mess with scary men and she'd stay off that Trump one. Something more benign like Christian Mingle or eHarmony. She'd be careful. "I'll get me a fireman," she said, "and he'll have a hunky fireman friend, and you and me, we'll have some fun."

A FEW DAYS later Elaine left Palm Garden Apartments to live with her father in nearby Seal Beach, because he unexpectedly had a stroke while lifting weights at the local YMCA. She would never say it, but his half-paralyzed face, slurred speech, walker, bleary eyes, and shaking hands gave her direction and meaning; the shattering dependability of death granting buoyancy and urgency to its flipside: life. Plus her scarlet *A* faded with a newfound nobility of purpose. Hyaluronidase injections quickly returned her face, dissolving some of the filler, and she did look rejuvenated and younger, but not brazenly so, as if someone had pressed refresh on a computer, making an image sharper.

Elaine felt certain she'd not see Serena again, no emails or phone numbers exchanged. They embraced for the first and last time before Elaine left, Serena careful not to press against Elaine's swollen and pained face. Then Serena handed her a parting gift: the brick. Yet Serena's presence continued to lodge outside of Elaine like a halo, disquieting and unshakable, a silent, imaginary, and angrily optimistic witness.

Elaine's time at Palm Gardens had lasted less than two months, but it seemed timeless, like a hex lingering in an extended sensation of uncertainty and transience. Confusions, shifting identities, anxiety, and poor judgment, cast in a never-ending blue of pool and sky and the yellow-lit Hi-Life Liquor sign, with a smell deep inside her nostrils: chlorine, marijuana, unidentified cooking spices, and an overriding antiseptic cleanser. Serena's music—classic rock—sifting in and out: Stevie Nicks, Billy Joel. One night Guns N' Roses' "Paradise City" over and over—*Take me down to the Paradise City, where the grass is green and the girls are pretty. Oh, won't you please take me home, yeah yeah*—until Elaine had gone through the brick-parted patio gate and asked a very stoned Serena to turn it off.

VISITATIONS

No one in her family talked about Grandpa Lewis. It was like he was dead. So when Rachel found him at Horizons Treatment Center, it was a shock, and she couldn't help but think it had been preordained. Her friend Dawn's father had been admitted to Horizons over the weekend for an addiction to painkillers. On Monday Dawn asked Rachel to come with her to visit him. Of course, Rachel said. They were JV doubles partners and had become close friends. As soon as fifth period ended, they met behind the quad and skipped algebra—a substitute teacher, easy to ditch— and Dawn drove them from Santa Monica to Malibu, where the rehab was located. The rehab was on a mountain, the road winding and shaded with trees. A pathway led from the parking lot to a Mediterranean-style structure: red terra-cotta roof, frosting-like cream-colored stucco walls, tiled steps, columns, and arched windows. It looked like a mansion and had a view of the Pacific spread under the sun like a sparkling blue blanket.

Rachel followed Dawn through the sliding glass doors. There was a giant flower arrangement like in a fancy restaurant or hotel, and it smelled clean and fresh. "Welcome," said a man sitting behind a desk. He stood, introduced himself—Todd, thirty-something: tan, blond, fit, probably a surfer in recovery—and discussed the situation with Dawn. Dawn's father, a big sweaty man, reminded Rachel of a fat seal, and she knew both he and Dawn blamed his ongoing back problems for his pill addiction. Dawn's parents were divorced, and though Dawn lived with her mother, she preferred her blustery and neglectful father. Who could blame her? He'd bought her a BMW last month for her sixteenth birthday. Rachel's father had died when she was three, and she could barely remember him. Visitation time had ended, but Todd said he'd make an exception and take Dawn to her father's room. "Only family," he said, and Rachel said she'd wait.

While Rachel waited, she wandered the corridors and peeked in the kitchen, which smelled like roast beef. A dry-erase board listed the patients' names and dietary restrictions, and that was when she saw her grandfather's name, with the stipulation that he was a vegetarian. She stared for some time. It took her a few minutes to adjust to the idea that her mother's father was here. You couldn't make it up. In a film or novel, she wouldn't have believed it. But life was like that. Lewis Aiden Powell. Grandpa

Lewis. She knew that he'd lived in Malibu at one point, and that he'd had a problem with alcohol and gambling. It must be him. He was almost never discussed, especially in front of her mother, who considered her stepfather—Poppa Dan—to be her real father and Rachel's grandfather. As far as Rachel could remember, she'd not met Grandpa Lewis, while Poppa Dan had always been active in their lives. It struck Rachel as incredible that she, too, was a vegetarian, the only one in her family besides, now she knew, Grandpa Lewis.

Outside at the patio a group of people sat around a table, their chairs pushed back. Behind them was a pool. A few smoked, and they seemed relaxed and pleased with themselves. A man in a tracksuit beckoned her. She approached them, and a woman asked if she was looking for someone. After she said her grandfather's name, they laughed, and then the woman said, "Oh, honey, are you sure?"

"He's my grandpa," Rachel said, heat rising to her cheeks.

"Room six," said another woman in a bored monotone, reaching to ash her cigarette. She added, "Down the hall to the left."

Rachel found the room and stood outside the door, listening. There was no noise, so she knocked gently. After some time, she opened the door.

Her grandpa slept, his mouth parted, and he made a wheezy breathing noise. A window with gauzy curtains gave the room a hazy golden light. An IV connected his left arm to a sagging plastic drip of clear fluid. His face looked similar to hers, angular and long, and his ears stuck out, same as hers. She hated this feature in herself and hid her ears behind her long hair, but it somehow made her feel protective of him. He was mostly bald, gray stubble at the sides of his head, and his closed eyelids looked wet and greased. His skin had a yellow pallor, and his arms and hands were speckled with age spots. The sheet and blanket were tucked around his body, molding his skinny frame, a small mound at his pelvic area. Old people usually repulsed her, like when her mom would make her kiss her great-aunt Lola, and she had that same visceral reaction. She was about to shut the door and leave, when he opened his eyes and stared at her. He seemed afraid, so she said, "I'm your granddaughter, Rachel."

It took him a minute, but then a smile spread across his face— seductive and sly—and he adjusted the bed upward, propping himself to a sit position, and said, "Well, I'll be," reaching out his other hand.

She came forward and took it, dry and cool, his fingers thin. She felt that familiar old-people repulsion, but also an instant connection and familiarity, like greeting a piece of herself; and there was also a sense of awe, due to the vacuum he'd created in the family, and the mystery that surrounded him. It was like meeting a mythological figure.

She thought briefly of her mother, grandmother, and Poppa Dan, and imagined herself at church with them, standing in the pew and singing, which she found dully comforting.

Grandpa Lewis asked how she'd found him. After she explained, he said, "Fate. Don't tell anyone," he added. "They won't understand."

She sat in a chair by his bed and they watched each other. The gauzy curtains fluttered behind him with the breeze, and a red hummingbird feeder hung from an awning.

"I'm dying," he said, nodding to the IV.

"But this isn't a hospital," she said.

"They like my money," he said. His lashes had stuck at the corners from his gunky eyes. He told her to look in the bedside table drawer. She did so, and found a leather key chain with a Mercedes symbol on it. "Take it," he said. "I'll tell you where it's parked. That way you can come back."

"Why," she asked, emboldened, "doesn't my mom talk to you?"

He looked down. She saw his chest lift and fall in a sigh. Then he glanced up and said, "Have you asked her?"

"She doesn't tell me anything." It was true. She knew her mom loved her, but she was inscrutable, especially about her past. Her chest tightened, as it sometimes did when she thought about her mom.

His eyebrows rose and a slight forced smile came to his lips. "I'll tell you," he said, "all about your mom."

Her phone buzzed with a text from Dawn.

Coming, she texted back.

She told him she'd visit again to hear his stories, and that she couldn't take his car. "I don't see why not," he said, and his hand rose from the bed. "No one needs to know." She stood, bent over him, but then decided not to kiss him. He smelled faintly of vinegar, though she didn't find it especially unappealing.

On the car drive back to Santa Monica, Rachel was careful to wait for Dawn to finish talking about her father. Then she told her about Grandpa Lewis. Dawn parked her BMW at the curb in front of Rachel's house to give her time to talk. Rachel explained that Grandpa Lewis had deserted his family when Rachel's mother was twelve. Rachel's grandma used to say that he'd run away from home, a coward. Grandma had met Poppa

Dan soon after at church, and that was also when Grandma and Mom had become born-again Christians. While Rachel felt stifled and bored in church, Grandma and Mom seemed to need it. Poppa Dan was a tax accountant and he'd raised Rachel's mom, and now she worked for him. Grandpa Lewis had been a brilliant businessman. He had the Midas touch, but apparently he'd screwed the family out of a fortune (they'd all be quite rich if it weren't for him) and his own brother—Uncle Rodney—had killed himself over money. Rachel didn't understand the extent, and it all seemed complicated and murky, but she knew that her family resented Grandpa Lewis's greater wealth, and she intuited that their moderate prosperity was considered morally superior. Over the years Grandpa Lewis's vices and addictions had been alluded to—gambling, sex, drugs, alcohol—although she'd not heard specifics, and she'd always wondered how he could remain rich. Didn't gambling and alcoholism equal destitution? It didn't make sense, and secretly she'd decided that there were two sides, and that she didn't hate him like the rest of her family did. Grandpa Lewis didn't come to family functions or occasions—even to funerals and marriages—and it was like he wasn't allowed or invited, though no one ever said that. Other relatives she didn't know would appear—distant cousins, nephews, nieces, uncles, aunts—but never Grandpa Lewis. Sometimes she'd overhear them asking about him with perverse curiosity, as if expecting the worst or gossiping about a celebrity. "I heard," one of them would say, "that he spent time in Malaysia and has another girlfriend." "I don't know where he is," Grandma would answer, "and frankly I don't care. Maybe he's dead."

When Rachel had finished talking, Dawn agreed not to tell

anyone about Grandpa Lewis, but added: "Be careful. He sounds manipulative."

Rachel went inside and found the shoebox of photographs her mom kept in her closet. Her mom wasn't home yet—it was tax season and she was working late with Poppa Dan at the office—and her grandma, who lived close by and often came over, wasn't there either. A note from her mom on the kitchen table told Rachel that there was lasagna in the refrigerator that she could heat up, and that Grandma would stop by to check on her. Rachel locked her bedroom door and then turned the box of photographs over on her bed, spreading them out on her bedspread. She didn't want to look at the photographs of herself as a baby and as a child, especially the ones with her dad in them, so she quickly placed those in a pile without looking closely. There weren't many, as most of her life had been documented digitally. Then she found several photographs of her mother as a baby with Grandma and Grandpa Lewis looking stylish and smiling happily. Grandma wore pencil skirts and dresses, her hair curled, and Grandpa Lewis wore suits and had all of his hair. Some were black-and-white, and the color ones had faded. Mom had her serious mom face but as a baby. Strange how she could see her mom, grandma, and grandpa in these images, but it wasn't who they were now. But it was too: they were inside these younger versions and faintly recognizable. Then there were the photos of her mom as a kid at five and six, until about ten. In all of these that included her mother's father, Grandpa Lewis's face had been cut, his head erased. Someone—her mom or grandma—had carefully used the scissors. But why only these and not when her mom was a baby and toddler? What had Grandpa done to warrant his meticulous removal? It was sad. Waving, standing, sitting, walking, a gap where his head should be, his torso headless, something vicious about not removing the entirety of him, like a repeated beheading.

THE NEXT DAY Rachel asked Dawn if she could go with her to Horizons. This time they didn't ditch and left after tennis practice. It wasn't visitation time, but Todd made an exception again. Grandpa Lewis had explained that Rachel was his granddaughter. Rachel found out that Grandpa Lewis had hepatitis C, along with other problems, and though he'd exaggerated by saying he was dying, it was true that he was quite sick. Todd said Horizons would bend the rules: she'd be allowed visitations whenever. She had the impression this also had to do with Grandpa Lewis's money. They arrived an hour before dinnertime. Dawn went to her father's room, and Rachel to her grandfather's.

"You came to your senses," Grandpa Lewis said when he saw her, "and returned for my car." His expression was satisfied.

"I'm fifteen," she said. "I don't have my license."

He shrugged. "Take it anyway," he said.

She sat, and he asked her questions about her life. He wanted to know her interests and political beliefs, and when she said she wanted to direct movies, he didn't laugh. No one in her family took her aspirations seriously, as if they were impractical and delusional dreams she'd grow out of. He knew who Sofia Coppola was (her favorite director), and the movies she mentioned, and he had thoughtful opinions. He read! No one in her family read.

She asked questions about her mom, and he told her what he remembered. "How'd she get that scar?" she asked.

"The big one on her chin? She didn't tell you?"

"She said she fell," she answered, and then reminded him: "She tells me nothing."

He laughed. Then he told her how when her mom was five, one of the neighbor kids had dared her to dive in a pool. She'd showed off and dived in the shallow end, hitting her chin. "She was a daredevil. A real tomboy."

Rachel couldn't picture it. She said, "She's not anymore, that's for sure."

At one point a hummingbird flittered at the feeder and he noticed her watching and turned to glance; then he faced her and said: "Those little buggers are among the cruelest of the bird species."

She didn't believe him and said, "But they're so cute."

"Get three or four of them at the feeder," he said, "and watch them fight."

She visited him all that week. When Dawn didn't want to drive, she took the bus. It wasn't that hard; she only had to walk a mile or so. She asked Grandpa Lewis questions, and he took his time answering. She asked about his history, and his narrative matched her grandmother's: tangled in a web of addictions, he'd irretrievably messed up. But in his version, and in the way that he told it—with humor, earnestness, sadness, somberness, and self-deprecation— she felt bad for him as well. He'd obviously thought a lot about it and had regrets. Addiction, she knew, was a disease. It wasn't like he wanted to be sick. The past didn't seem as horrific, and he certainly wasn't unforgivable. "Of course," he said at one point, "your grandmother and mother have differing versions. You can't ever really know the truth, just like you can't ever really know what happens to another person, or what they think happened to them, which becomes the same thing." He was funny and could mimic her grandmother's voice and gestures—she laughed out loud—but he didn't do so in a mean-spirited way. She discovered a few family secrets: her grandmother had been engaged before Grandpa Lewis to his best friend. There'd been two other suicides in their family, one of them Grandma's sister's husband. She also learned that her dad, who'd died of cancer, had also been an alcoholic. Before he'd died and without her mom's knowledge, he'd met with Grandpa Lewis, and brought Rachel, no more than two years old at the time, so that Grandpa could also meet his granddaughter.

"A good man," Grandpa said.

The room seemed to tilt. "I don't remember," Rachel said.

"He loved you."

"I don't remember him."

"That's okay," Grandpa said.

The next afternoon Rachel asked Grandpa Lewis why the family blamed and ostracized him. Was it jealousy? Was it because of his brother's suicide? Had he stolen their money? She didn't understand.

Grandpa Lewis gave her a deep stare and said, "I cut all ties."

"Why?"

"Who wants to be judged," he said—a statement, not a question.

"Don't you miss them?"

"Nah," he said. His hand went up and he continued, "I don't want a family."

She felt her eyes widening. It seemed inconceivable.

"You're shocked," he said. "Don't be. One day you'll under-stand. You're not like them. I've known all along."

A shiver went through her. She took her elbows in her hands and pressed her arms against her chest. She was pleased that Grandpa Lewis thought she was intelligent and special. She *was* different from her family. They had numerous faults and settled for so little. Grandpa Lewis preferred her. But at the same time she didn't want to be different. It scared her. She wanted their approval, even if they bored her. She wanted to be normal, to get married someday and have children. Sure, she'd be an artist, too, and she was attracted to unusual people. But she didn't want to end up in a rehab that was like a high-end spa, without family, paying for people to defer to her.

Grandpa Lewis reached for her hand. She held his hand and, after some time, she leaned forward and pressed her lips against his jaw. It wasn't the first time that they'd touched or kissed— they'd grown affectionate, especially when saying goodbyes, and she'd gotten completely over her old-people repulsion with him—but there seemed to be a newfound intimacy. She thought about her dad bringing her to meet Grandpa Lewis. How he'd wanted them to have a relationship. Maybe her dad had been different, too. They continued to hold hands for a few more minutes, even when Todd came in the room and adjusted her grandpa's IV. When Todd left, she asked Grandpa about his health.

"I'm dying," he repeated, his eyelids wet and yellow-gunked. "There's not much anyone can do. I'll get hospice. They'll let me stay here as long as I pay."

She used a Kleenex to wipe his eyes. Todd had said Grandpa wasn't dying, and she didn't know whom to believe.

He seemed to know what she was thinking, because he said, "It's hard to know who's telling the truth. It makes you wonder, what people say, what they want you to know, don't want you to know, how they tell their stories the way they want them to go, rather than what's true. What they cannot see, won't acknowledge."

She told him she couldn't visit over the weekend. It'd be too hard to do it without her family noticing.

He said, "I'll miss you," and she said she'd miss him, too.

She took his Mercedes this time, because she didn't want to deal with the crowded bus on a Friday. She told him she'd bring it back on Monday after school, and she told herself this, too. She wasn't really taking it.

He lifted his hand and said, "Keep it."

An enormous glittering Mercedes with tinted windows waited for her on the gravel under an awning. It was easy. She'd practiced enough in her mom's Toyota and knew how to maneuver. Everything was automatic and geared toward efficient luxury. It was silver-colored with a darker interior and much nicer than Dawn's BMW.

Driving slowly and carefully, she loved the amenities and the new-leather smell. She pulled off at a lookout, stopping for a while, listening to the radio, the ocean sparkling below and extending to the horizon in a glistening blur of water and sky. She couldn't resist taking selfies in the Mercedes, and she sent the best one to Dawn, texting: *G'pa L insisted.*

She couldn't find a parking place—Friday in Santa Monica,

and she couldn't park at her house—so she pulled into a liquor-store lot and texted Dawn again, who called and told her about a few hidden spaces behind their high school gym. They spoke for several minutes and Dawn expressed concern. "Don't worry," Rachel told her. "I'm giving it back."

"It's not that," Dawn said. "It's you. You're clueless. He's a sick man. There's a reason," she continued, "your family disowned him."

"He disowned them," she said.

On Sunday she went to church with her family. It was all so simplistic. Jesus died for our sins, blah, blah, let us worship. Thinking about the Mercedes made her feel powerful and elated. She'd driven it on Saturday night for hours, even on the freeway, while her mom thought she was at Dawn's. She stood and sang with her mom, her grandma, and Poppa Dan, the songs dumb and repetitive. *Let us praise him. He hath risen.* Her mom and grandma looked the same, fair-haired and sharp-featured, and they tilted their heads the same angle with matching beatific ex-pressions. Please, God, she thought, let me be different. Let me look and act like someone else. Poppa Dan always seemed a bit angry, but it was just the way his face was set. Her mom glanced at her, and she felt a familiar sadness flare. She didn't want to become like her mom: reticent, quiet, and somber. She thought of Grandpa Lewis mimicking her grandma. She'd much rather be with him in his room, talking about art and holding hands and watching the hummingbirds fight. He'd taught her that life could incline less toward an oppressive uniformity and more in the fertile direction of risk and excitement. She was grateful. A shot of anger went through her: How could they discard Grandpa Lewis? Whatever he'd done, how could it be that bad? Wasn't

Jesus about forgiveness? The reasons for exclusion seemed arbitrary. Not about morals or principles, but about fostering and rationalizing grievances and clan-like allegiances. Disgrace wasn't simple and it had no rules. She might be next.

After church they had a late breakfast at a coffee shop called Shakers, because Grandma was out of eggs. The restaurant was bustling and smelled like coffee and pancakes. Mom and Poppa Dan talked at length about taxes and clients. Grandma rolled her eyes in fun at Rachel and whispered as if telling a secret: "They complain every year. Ha." Her voice went normal, addressing Mom and Poppa Dan: "We're not fooled—you both love it," and they all laughed.

Rachel was quiet for most of the meal. But when the check came, she asked, "What did Grandpa Lewis do?" She made her face neutral and her voice light. "I mean," she continued, "why do we avoid him? I can never remember."

Her mom said, "Nothing. He did nothing. He was a nothing father," but she didn't sound angry and was looking around the restaurant in a distracted way.

Grandma scanned the check and then handed it to Poppa Dan, saying, "He acted like a real jerk. That's what he did."

Poppa Dan fiddled for his wallet. He eyed the check and said, "He didn't just act like a real jerk. He was and is a jerk." He peered over his reading glasses at Rachel and added, "But we have each other. And that's what counts."

AFTER SCHOOL AND tennis practice on Monday, Rachel drove the Mercedes to Horizons and parked it where Grandpa Lewis had. When she got to his room, she found him with an oxygen tube in his nostrils. He still had his IV. Fingering the tubing, he said, "You're here! I've missed you."

"Are you okay?" she asked. It upset her that he might be dying.

He smiled and said, "Come here," and his arm went up. She came to him and they held hands. With his other hand, he caressed her cheek. It felt relaxed and natural. She brushed her fingers across the tubing in his nose and then touched a small scratch at his nostril. "They need to be more careful," she said. The tips of his fingers slipped behind her hair at her neck. She leaned over him and kissed near his ear, his skin warm and scratchy.

Rachel heard her mom's voice in the hallway. Startled and confused, she stood. She heard Todd say something, and then her mom said, "He's dangerous. That's why," and Todd said, "I'm so sorry," and her mom said with despair, "I can't believe this. I can't believe this is happening." She glanced at her grandfather and he looked like a frightened child.

As soon as her mom and Todd entered, a silence fell over the room. There was only the wheeze of the oxygen tube. The air seemed heavy, as if Rachel could hold it. She saw pain in her mother's eyes, and her grandpa looked humiliated. "Mom," she said, "what is it?" Then she was able to answer for herself, because she knew: she had no other choice, no other story made sense. He'd touched her mom the way he was beginning to touch her, but much worse. She wasn't a hundred percent clear, but she understood enough. Her mom gripped her arm like she was three years old and pulled her toward the doorway. Just as they were leaving, Poppa Dan and Grandma came inside. Grandma stared at Grandpa Lewis. But she said, "Rachel Marie," using her middle name, so Rachel would know she was angry and disappointed with her, "you don't know anything. You don't know what you've done. Dawn told your mom this afternoon. She's a good friend. This is bad, bad," and then to Grandpa Lewis, her eyes still directed at him: "You're an infection."

Poppa Dan was holding Grandma's hand and he said, "Easy now."

Grandma shook her hand free. "What's wrong with you?" she spat out at Grandpa Lewis.

"If I knew," he said, "would I be here?"

Her mom led Rachel from the room, but she heard her grandma say, "Sure. Sure you would. You know exactly what's wrong, but you can't stop yourself."

THAT NIGHT RACHEL watched the rain outside her bedroom window, the light around the streetlights hanging in copper flecks. Her mom had told her that she'd explain everything soon. But for now, they both needed to calm down. Rachel locked her door and then dragged the shoebox out from under her bed. In the dim light, she sorted through the photos again, pulling out all the headless ones. After arranging them on her bedspread in chronological order, she tried imagining what had happened. The air got heavy again, like it had in Grandpa Lewis's room.

The next morning, Rachel ditched and took the bus to Horizons. She'd forgotten to give back the Mercedes key. She waited until Todd wasn't at the desk, and then she slipped inside to Grandpa Lewis's room. He had his oxygen and IV and looked tired and surprised to see her. When she told him she was never coming back, his face distorted into something like grief. She held his hand one last time. At first what she felt was simply her skin pressed against his. But then that familiar sensation came— love, connection, understanding—and something else now, a shame between them. "I'm sorry," he said. "Really I am." She saw the tears glittering in his eyes and decided not to give him back the key. A sense that this was what it meant to grow up came over her. She'd created an imaginary version of Grandpa Lewis. Whatever she'd believed, whatever it was she thought she could control, she now understood was beyond her scope, that irrespective of what stories she told herself, she could never see—as Poppa Dan liked to say—more than through a glass darkly. Then she remembered her mom's frightened face as they sat in the car in the Horizons parking lot. Her mom was shivering. Rachel saw that she would have to comfort her, telling her then, as she reached and touched her fingers to her mom's forearm, and as her mom had told a younger Rachel many times: "There's nothing to be afraid of. I love you."

APPETITE

Claire and I met at a party to celebrate the launch of her husband's second book. My husband and I had moved from Colorado Springs to Los Angeles two years earlier, and an unsophisticated aura surrounded us, having both been raised in conventional middle-class Republican families. There was a certain type at parties like this: intellectual, vocally liberal, slightly bohemian, creative and with good taste, and quietly and mysteriously moneyed. I was watchful and impressed.

My husband, Jeff, taught history at a high school, most of his free time consumed by a yearbook commitment he'd been pressured into taking, and I was on maternity leave from a secretarial position, though I'd quit soon to stay home with our newborn son, David. Jeff had heard about the party through a friend who hadn't shown, and there was no one else we knew.

Displayed on a stand at a table where the book was being sold, *Material Promises* was over seven hundred pages long, the cover a profile photograph of a somber and bearded and younger Richard, fist at his chin. Published by an academic press associated with the private college where he taught, his books were classified as experimental fiction. At that time I admired anyone who'd crossed that impenetrable threshold to publication, and I hoped to meet him, though I didn't yet want to think of myself as ambitious.

Richard sat at the corner of the living room, and I passed David—less than one month old—to Jeff. I made myself walk over. Though Richard gazed the other direction, an almost imperceptible tug at his mouth led me to believe that he knew I was there. I opened my lips to speak, but in near synchronicity his head went back and his eyes closed and then he touched his eyelids with his fingertips as if in distress, so I retreated.

"Did you talk to him?" Jeff asked.

I grimaced, letting him know that he was no better at networking than I, and I took back our fussing son.

"Over an hour left," I whispered, shaking my head no, because, wide-eyed, Jeff had gestured to the front door. We'd agreed to last at least two hours at the party.

Later I was breastfeeding David on a couch in a private den, listening to his *mmm-hmm-mmm* sound, his little leg poked out from the blanket that enclosed him at my chest, when I saw Claire studying a small landscape painting near the open door. She wore a simple black dress and absentmindedly fingered her jade choker, her hiccupping daughter in a BabyBjörn facing her chest, splotchy legs and arms wobbling with each hiccup. Claire looked closer—and closer still—until it appeared her nose might touch the painting.

I knew she was married to Richard even though she was younger, because I'd watched them earlier. She was affected with him and vice versa: they seemed to encourage it like a performance, both using the words "my love" with a condescending edge and an unnerving frequency. ("Pass me my drink, my love." "Of course, my love. Here you are, my love." "Thank you, my love.") She was pale and elegant, and I wondered how she remained so passionately thin—her figure like a boy's—when, like me, she'd recently given birth.

Even before she turned and saw us—with a surprised step back and a smile—I knew that she and her daughter would join us at the couch. And she did, unhooking Lily from her carrier and propping her forward on her lap with one hand at Lily's chest and neck, tapping at Lily's back with the other. "Beautiful," she said, glancing back at the painting. "The rest"—she gave a dismissive hand wave, while still supporting her daughter.

"Isn't this your house?" I asked.

"Oh, hell no," she said in amusement, and then added seriously, "It belongs to a colleague of Richard's."

For a long while we silently watched Lily bobble with each hiccup, a bubble of saliva forming at her bottom lip. The only other sound was the rhythmic patting of Claire's palm against

Lily's back and David's breastfeeding hum. Then Lily's hiccups stopped and soon her head drooped in sleep.

Claire placed her on the couch between us, with Lily's tiny arms and legs splayed. Claire and I shared notes: ages of babies (Lily three weeks older than David), our ages (both of us in our late twenties), and our birthing experiences (still viscerally recent and traumatic).

Then David drifted to sleep, his mouth barely tugging at my nipple, little ticklish nibbles. His leg shook outside the blanket, a convulsive twitch, and then he stilled, his mouth fully releasing my nipple and his leg and body leaden against me.

With both our babies asleep, our conversation became deeper, freighted, based on the profundity and strangeness of new motherhood and our mutual need for companionship. We talked about how we'd been mothered (hers a competitive, intellectual Episcopalian, mine an anti-intellectual born-again Christian), and how long-buried memories of our childhoods now came unbidden and unwanted. She paraphrased Germaine Greer, saying that once a woman has a child, her capacity for suffering deepens. We agreed that what we felt for our newborns was larger and more passionate than any love affair. Our marriages, our first loves, and our closest familial relationships paled. And how, after we'd given birth, we'd both felt an uncanny awareness as if we were, as she phrased it, "at the center of an abyss."

FOR YEARS MY son and I went to Claire's on Tuesday and Thursday afternoons, because Richard had late classes and she and Lily wanted the company. We'd stay for dinner and leave before bedtime, after Claire and I had bathed our children. Her home was like an art project (especially compared to our apartment): a porcelain tiger perched near the bathtub, a wooden bowl filled with antique dice, a thick curtain used as a tablecloth, tomatoes sprouting in her garden, a church pew transformed into a bench. I'd never met a woman with such assurance, and it seemed to me that Claire was a true artist: her life was her art. Though I never did figure out where she and Richard got their money—surely not from Richard's salary or book sales—I learned from Claire's discernment and style.

Often we would talk at her kitchen table while feeding our babies, and she'd sit stiff-backed, her posture impeccable. She'd been a ballerina forced to quit due to a knee injury. Once in a while she'd demonstrate a plié or show me how she could stand on her toes, but that was rare. She had an air of defeat, of troubles endured, and of privilege.

I told her that I'd been promiscuous in high school and throughout college, and that I'd settled into marriage and the accompanying monogamy with relief. She told me that she'd been proposed to twice. She'd slept with these men and two others. She'd been Richard's student in graduate school, affairs common at this college.

A studio next to the garage was hers, and she painted minuscule abstracts layered with opaque paints that took months to dry; they never seemed to be done. Their lives, she explained with a note of disdain and impatience, revolved around Richard's art. While she complained about his lack of involvement on the home front, she also relished the role of expert on all things domestic and child related.

She fed me tofu stir-fry, grilled shrimp and asparagus, coconut macaroons, homemade vanilla-bean ice cream, puddings, and stews. Not to mention the leftover snacks and meals set out for our kids that I ended up finishing: peanut butter and jelly sandwiches, buttered popcorn, salt-and-vinegar potato chips. I snacked and ate and gained weight, until Jeff commented, and I began to monitor my eating.

She also gave me books, most from Richard's library (Henry James and Samuel Beckett her favorites), saying I could keep them; he wouldn't notice. I have a shelf comprising over thirty books from Claire.

Once she told me, "I watch you take things in, and I can tell that you remember everything you see and hear. You're the real deal, Lauren." Another time: "I feel like you were supposed to meet me and that your writing life led you here."

When our kids got a little older, Claire turned most of her studio into a play area, saying that someday she'd convert the entire space back into her ideal studio. She even had plans drawn up by an architect.

Sometimes she'd look at me, understanding that what I wanted most was time to write, and she'd say, "Go," and I'd write in there for a couple of hours while she watched our kids elsewhere.

I'd work at a red toddler-sized table, cramped in a corner with the toys, my foot touching a Big Wheel, because I felt more comfortable in the play area than at her desk near her unfinished paintings.

Afterward Claire and I would watch cartoons and movies with our children, sitting on the couch in her dark living room in a zombie-like stupor, piles of unfolded laundry surrounding us.

Lily's little hand would sometimes reach up and caress my ear-lobe—the feeling probably reminded her of being in the womb—mistaking me as her mom. Her face would turn to see me in the glow of the television. A small shudder of surprise, but then her lips would lift around her pacifier in a shy smile, and she'd continue to stroke my earlobe, her eyes going back to the screen and her mouth resuming its soft reassuring *suck-suck-suck* at her binky.

ONE AFTERNOON OUTSIDE Souplantation, I was telling Claire about my sex dream—this time with a chef from the cooking channel—when David, chasing Lily around a fountain, slipped and fell. A flash of light went through me, as if I were also falling. But long after, when I knew that there would be no concussion or stitches, and after I'd concluded that I'd been at fault but not in a wretched way, a bewildering sensation—like a vibration laced with danger and helplessness—continued to course through me. Though it was related to the fall and to that frightening link be-tween David and me, and, more generally, between parents and their children, I knew that what I felt was mostly a premonition having to do with Claire.

Earlier we'd had a messy smorgasbord self-serve lunch.

"I don't want to be one of those moms," Claire had said in a distracted voice, expounding on a common theme, placing a napkin in her daughter's lap. "Tired, rumpled clothes, fat. Every vomit and spit-up and crap important. Planning meals: sliced wienies and grapes."

"Their kids more talented, smarter," I said, thinking about how Claire prepared meals for our children, slicing their tofu dogs into non-choke-able pieces, making sure they had servings of vegetables and fruits.

"Geniuses," she said, steadying Lily's hand, which had swiped her napkin to the floor. "So many little geniuses, everywhere."

Claire enjoyed watching me eat, and the remnants of multi-colored frozen yogurt dollops, bread rolls with hardened butter pats, and relish-speckled potato salad surrounded me on the table.

I ate well whenever I was with her: it was our routine. I gave her an unchallenged notion of herself, a reassuring sense of admiration, and a padding that extended around her and hid her from the outside world; and in exchange, she nourished me.

I told her stories. I'd find myself embellishing, fattening a fresh drama or anecdote or dream. I'd wait for the right moment (the kids quietly immersed in coloring books or a video) and then present it, making her smile and laugh (though not always, which was the challenge). There has always been great pleasure for me in making a sad person momentarily happy.

Claire wasn't eating, blaming her lack of appetite on spastic bowel syndrome, and her eyes had a glassy look from the Percocet she'd taken earlier for her migraine.

I'd learned to view her illnesses as she did—as essential to her, like another part of her personality. Her doctor visits and the various misdiagnoses, medications, and tests filled her with both disdain and pleasure; a stupid remark from a doctor would please her immensely.

When she reached over the table for an extra napkin, her blouse gaped open, and I averted my gaze, but not soon enough: I saw her chest caved inward at her sternum, her ribs visible.

"What's wrong?" she asked, because I must have made a face.

"Who's ready to go?" I said, making my voice cheery.

"Me, me!" David said, his butt lifting and falling from his booster chair.

"Me!" said Lily. "Me, me!"

THE FOLLOWING THURSDAY, Richard came home early and Claire gave him a look, so that I knew she'd told him to talk to me about my writing. She took the kids to decorate the sidewalk with colored chalks, leaving Richard and me in the living room. She'd made us root beer floats, and Richard stirred his with a spoon that clinked against his glass. His legs were long and he sat with them crossed.

"What do you want to write, Lauren?" he asked, and already he seemed bored. I imagined him dealing with students all afternoon, and then having to come home to his wife's doting friend. I wondered if he knew I was writing about sippy cups and potty training.

"I want to write like Bukowski," I said, because that was the first thing that came to mind. "Like fire," I continued, "even if I make people mad."

He laughed, and for the first time he really looked at me, as if he'd been expecting me to say something boring, but I'd surpassed his expectation by saying something stupid. "Sorry," he said, still laughing, and he shook his head a little, his hand going to his forehead, having trouble stifling his amusement. "It's nothing," he said, chuckling. "I'm sorry."

"That's okay," I said, my face hot.

"Sorry," he said, "sorry, sorry. There. All done." He raised a hand in the air. "No more. See. All done."

"Bukowski wasn't a mom," I said.

"No, no," he said. "It's not that." He paused and set his glass on the side table. "Bukowski?" he said with contempt. "Drunk, sloppy." He made air quotes with his fingers. "One of the people."

"Honest, real"—I couldn't think. "Have you read his poetry?"

"I can't help you," he said, turning to look at the *Nation* magazine near his glass on the side table.

I stood and made my way to the bathroom, where I splashed cold water on my face. There was shock and humiliation, but even more so, I felt invigorated.

Later Claire made the two of us gin and tonics with ice and limes. "If you were Richard," she said, when we were on our second, "you'd write about me. He's got a gold mine but writes things that don't matter, and then says no one's smart enough to understand."

She mimicked a droning male voice—probably Richard's: "'Using real people and factual material is dishonest and exploitative.'"

She stared at me so that I understood she knew I filled my notebooks with details about our time. Maybe she could tell by the way I watched her and our children, weighing what they said and how they looked and moved, thinking how I might use it. Whole sentences would form, word for word, and if I didn't get the chance to write at Claire's, as soon as I'd strapped David into his car seat, I'd mumble the sentences aloud until we got home, and then rush to get David settled so that I could scribble them down before forgetting.

We heard music and laughter from the living room, where our kids were watching cartoons. "Women are like dogs," Claire said, a cottony white saliva extending at the corner of her mouth, probably from mixing her medications with alcohol.

I wanted to take a wet paper towel to her face.

"Love me," she said in a pitiful voice. "Pet me, admire me, feed me."

She rested her arms on the kitchen table, bony and lined with veins, hands cupping her glass; her knuckles stuck out.

"Richard underestimates you," she said, "but I don't."

She took a sip and made a sour expression. "Let him," she added. "Stop being a doggie and find out what happens."

A FEW MONTHS later Claire and I sat on her porch drinking iced teas while Lily and David sprinted naked through the revolving sprinklers set on her front lawn. They took wild leaps, squealed with glee, and fell and rolled. They ran—blades of grass stuck to their backs and behinds—specks of glistening water raining over them. Claire and I usually shared our appreciation with silent looks, but when I glanced over, she looked away.

Later we went for a walk to visit our tree on the block next to hers—an old oak with a bend in the trunk where the kids liked to sit.

David's shoelace was untied, and he turned from me to Claire. When it came to anything practical, he preferred her quiet efficiency.

After David had caught up with Lily, Claire looked at me with an expression of determination. "Richard and his friends," she said, and she paused. "*Our* friends," she amended. "I have to say this, Lauren, I really do."

She turned her attention to our kids climbing the oak.

"Listen," she said, "because I'll only say this once." She laughed unhappily, shook her head, laughed some more, her eyes on our kids. "You're going to accomplish what they never will, Lauren. What *we* never will. They think they're talented, think they're geniuses, and that fucks an artist. You and me—we can't stay friends."

I tried to protest but she said, "Yeah, yeah, I know, yeah, yeah, it's sad. But that's beside the point. I'll eat my foot if I'm not right."

THE FOLLOWING WEEK David had the flu. I got sick and another week passed. Then it was Claire and Lily's turn. Everyone healthy by the next Tuesday, our routine resumed.

The kids and I had finished our mac and cheese, and they'd gone to the living room, leaving Claire and me in the kitchen.

Claire was at the sink to wash dishes and I was next to her to dry, when Claire looked at me and instead of noticing my desire and saying, "Go," she said, "You know what? I can't babysit while you write anymore." She added, "I don't want to be a part of your process."

I felt certain that this wasn't coming from her, that Richard had spoken through her (my process?), and I let this show in my expression.

She turned from me to rinse a bowl and added: "I read your notebook. You left your purse open."

I felt like she'd sucker punched me. The notebook was mostly blank, thankfully—I'd only recently bought it, having filled up the last one. I'd scribbled a few sentences about what I'd eaten and described some plants and the sky—and one small detail about Claire's wedding ring, which she'd masking-taped around the rim to stay on her bony finger.

"My process," I said, managing to keep my voice calm, "is mine. It doesn't need your—or anyone else's—approval."

We were both unaccustomed to my speaking out, as if our roles had switched and I was instructing her.

By the time we spoke again, it was pleasantries while we bathed our kids, yet everything seemed grim and changed.

ON A THURSDAY afternoon not long after, Richard opened the front door. "Claire will be back any minute," he said. David followed Lily to her room, leaving Richard and me alone. He'd been cycling and still wore an aerodynamic helmet and crotch-padded tight shorts, and his biking shoes clinked on the linoleum as he moved through the kitchen.

He was gracious, offering me a cappuccino, which he made from a gleaming silver European espresso machine that he loved. I was glad when he removed his helmet, placing it on the table next to the salt and pepper shakers.

We were engaged in awkward conversation when his cell phone rang. By the way he lowered his voice and turned his back, I knew that it was Claire, and that something bad had happened.

He murmured into the phone as if comforting a child. I got up to leave, lifting from my chair, but he looked back and gestured for me to sit.

After he hung up, he sat next to me at the kitchen table. He explained that Claire had driven the wrong way in a parking lot and had slashed the tires. She was Lyft-ing home now, and he thought it best if David and I weren't there when she returned. I agreed. He looked down at his hands and there were blotches of pink at his cheeks. A heavy silence developed, and he appeared haunted and vulnerable and sad. I wanted to ask about the spastic bowel syndrome, the unending migraines, the anorexia. The Percocet and Xanax and Darvocet.

"She's sick," he said.

I nodded.

"She thinks you're going to write about her. Don't."

"Why don't you?" I said, emboldened.

He winced, staring at his hands again, and then he looked at me as if I were very sick instead of Claire.

"I'd rather keep my marriage," he said. "Thanks anyway."

We sat quietly for several moments. I wondered about my health and Claire's sickness, how I got stronger and more confident while she became progressively worse. For a moment I imagined myself as a parasitic, ballooning animal sucking off Claire's shrinking body.

As David and I left, I caught a glimpse of myself in the hallway mirror. My face had a bloated, frightened look and though I felt fragile, I noticed a predatory gleam to my eyes.

A FEW WEEKS later, Claire arranged a dinner party and insisted that I come, saying that she wanted me to meet other writers. We'd not socialized before—our relationship private and protected and limited by our children—both of us preferring it that way, so this was a first. Jeff didn't want to go, so I went by myself.

Claire wore a pearl-colored slip dress, her hipbones protruding from the material and her exposed clavicle reminding me of a clothes hanger. Silver bracelets clinked up and down her arm. Her hair was up, her neck long. I wore jeans and a soft cotton shirt that she'd given me.

Two novelists and a poet arrived and ignored me. I let most of the dialogue go past me, nodding or smiling only when someone looked at me, concentrating instead on how to leave without seeming rude.

"All I'm saying," Richard said at one point with an air of patience, "is that everything after Leopold Bloom is crap."

We were at the dinner table, and Claire had served us baby spinach salads with goat cheese and roasted beets. "That's right, my love," she said. Her eyes flashed and she folded her hands at the table. "Go on. Tell us."

"It's simple," he said, pausing to fork beets into his mouth. He chewed aggressively, swallowed. "Leopold Bloom," he said, "ate with relish the inner organs of beasts and fowl." He smiled directly at me and then continued, "He liked thick giblet soup, nutty gizzards, a stuffed roast heart."

"A person of appetites," Claire said. "Like Lauren."

"He liked grilled mutton kidneys," Richard continued, "which gave to his palate a fine tang of faintly scented urine."

I was going to say something, possibly joke about how I didn't like the taste of urine, but then Lily, sleepy-eyed and in pajamas, came from the living room where she'd been watching television.

She stood next to me, her hand at my shoulder. I felt a surge of affection along with a sense of despair.

I looked at Claire, the expression on her face vivid, her stare deliberate and pointed, as though she hated me. No one else seemed to notice, and my gaze went to my lap; I kept my face downcast. Voices swirled around me and a coolness collected at my stomach.

When I finally glanced back at Claire, she returned a chastened expression, though I wonder now if I imagined this because I wished it so.

Lily went to her room, the dinner party continued, and I left early. Walking to my car, I wondered why I continued our friendship. I felt a sharp sensation, like something fierce and ravenous gnawing inside me, insisting on my freedom. What I had to do, I decided, was extract Claire from my life, like rooting out an infection.

David and I didn't show up on our visit days, and Claire didn't contact us, making me wonder if she'd orchestrated the separation. David and Lily had been growing apart anyhow, both starting kindergarten soon.

But then a few weeks passed and in an expansive mood, I tried to call Claire. She didn't return my messages.

The following month I thought I saw her near the grocery parking lot from a distance, struggling with a shopping cart, and as I walked toward her, my mouth stretched in a smile.

The person gave me a quizzical look, and as I got closer, I saw that she was a skinny young woman, no more than twenty-five. I helped her pull the shopping cart from the others and watched her leave.

Then over the holidays, Claire sent me a card: a delicately embossed handmade one; I sent her ours: puppies in a sleigh wearing Santa hats.

I called her last week and, surprisingly, she answered. She told me that I remain her emergency contact for Lily; and she's mine for David, because I trust her with his well-being like I trust no one else.

Our conversation inevitably led to a discussion of her decline: Her migraines have increased in strength, duration, and frequency, as has her accompanying drug consumption. She's losing clumps of hair; her gums are bleeding and receding. She suffers fatigues and debilitating sinus infections, and there will be more tests and brain scans with nothing discovered or resolved.

I offered to help, to drive her to doctor appointments—anything she needed, anything at all—but I knew that not only would she not take me up on it, but that this would also likely be the last time we talked.

"Don't worry," she told me at the end of our conversation. "I'm fine. Nothing," she continued, "will ever obliterate or devastate me, Lauren. You know that."

In obedience for my sake and hers, I pretended to believe her, because she nourished me and listened to me and laughed at my stories and we loved each other's children; and she elevated me and contributed to my resolve, so that because of Claire and in retaliation and respect to her downfall, I'll achieve the very same goals that before her I would not have dared to pursue.

Nobody's Business

Ben sat cross-legged, having woken a few minutes earlier in his mom's walk-in closet. He'd been kept warm by her clothes pulled loose from their hangers, and her jacket rolled into a ball had been his pillow. Last night, cocooned inside the closet, he'd gone on one of his private crying jags, the worst so far: limbs loose, eyes like rivers. Then he must've fallen asleep. Really, nothing surprised him anymore. He could barely hear the faint *whish* of the showerhead: Rita, the T days' caretaker (Tuesdays and Thursdays), bathing his mom in the bathroom down the hallway near the den. He pictured his mom hunched on the steel bench, a line of soap running down the bumps of her spine, her nipples surprisingly long. His cell phone buzzed in his pocket and he silenced it, knowing it was his father, who called every morning. Perfunctory conversations: high school, money, schedule. The worst was when his father would ask to speak to Ben's mom, and he'd try to hand her his cell phone, but she'd turn her head like a child refusing medicine. He wasn't up for it, but now he'd have to call his father back.

Ben knew his mom had been the third wife—the wife to have fun with, since his father already had two bitter exes and four daughters older than her. Ben, seven years old at the time, had been part of the package, and he'd wanted a father; fortunately Howard had wanted a son. Almost immediately Ben had called Howard "Father," like the position was a formal one—never "Dad" or "Daddy"—and Howard had called him "Son." But when Ben's mom got sick—really sick—eight years into the marriage, not just the arm and leg twitching and unexplainable falls, but after there was a name (ALS or Lou Gehrig's or the French *maladie de Charcot*) and right about the same time she could no longer drive the white Corvette, that was when Howard had moved to an apartment, abandoning her to the caretakers, and to Ben. She was cavalier and indifferent—dramatic eye rolls and sighs—when Howard visited or tried to kiss her, as if now that she was dying, she didn't have to pretend.

She'd been a model and had married Howard when the jobs had slowed. She'd make Ben laugh, whipping things (pieces of toast, her eyeliner pencil) at the photographs of her that Howard had put up around the house. In most, she had a seductive mocking expression, almost cruel. At her request the photos were now stacked facedown in the garage beside her tennis racquets. Ben probably loved Howard more than she did—if she loved him at all—and she wasn't angry with Howard for deserting them, which made it difficult for Ben to be mad. Also he knew he was privy to her inner life—the one Howard wanted to know and never would. Like his heartbeat, she was always there, and when he tried to imagine her dead, he could not.

Ben heard a yip, his mom accidentally hitting Peanut with her wheelchair again. The runty mutt wouldn't leave her side, not even to go outside and shit. Ben left the closet and went to his mom, opening the wood doors that separated the den from the hallway. He heard the swoosh and flap of Rita shaking out a sheet. Heavy closed curtains gave the room a timeless, dank feel, and along with the stink of urine, there was a medicinal smell. Paper towels blanketed the wood floor, covering the spots where Peanut had peed. His mother had named her wheelchair Tara because it was so big and expensive. She looked like a child driving a towering truck. Her eyes blazed at him. She couldn't eat much and barely talked anymore. But the hum in her eyes said that she knew that he'd slept in his clothes and had cried; regardless, she still wanted him to do what she'd told him to do last night, which was to put Peanut out of his misery. They'd been watching TV (an *I Love Lucy* marathon) in their usual connective stupor, when, out of nowhere, she'd made her request. Patches of dark showed in her robe where Rita hadn't dried her well enough—fuck, how many times did he have to tell these people to do it right? Peanut shivered on her lap, the pink tip of his fingernail-sized tongue poking out. He looked like a retarded rabbit. Tan—like a peanut—except for his black eyes and the darker, shaggy peach-colored fur around his mouth and asshole, the dog was losing his mind. The sicker she got, the worse he got. He snarled and snapped and had bitten Ben twice and nipped two of the caretakers. His mom grunted and raised a finger. The finality in her stare made Ben look away. Her eyes had become fiercer; he saw flashes of light sometimes.

She made a soft *coo* noise, and he looked back. Her hair was tangled and wet and he decided he might brush it. He could be late—he had P.E. first period and knew his teacher wouldn't mark him tardy. Like the other caretakers, Rita was inferior when it came to the details of caring for his mom. He watched her working to dribble a word out, a vein forking her forehead. "Peanut," she finally said. He nodded. She tapped her armrest—You, she was saying, it has to be you—and then her hand went back to its curl. Sometimes she wore his socks on her hands to keep them warm. Her eyes softened and she grimaced. "I don't need a shower," he said, and when she tapped again, he said, "Fine, I'll take one."

THEY'D GONE TO Fiji, Australia, New Zealand, Hawaii, Japan, for her modeling jobs when he was little, and she'd taught him to drive when he was six in Mexico, letting him sit on her lap and steer down the dusty, potholed streets. When he crapped his pants in the second grade, she'd told him to get used to it, that life was full of humiliations. Loss and heartbreak, too. But she said that hell was a made-up place, don't let anyone tell you different, and that nobody knew what happened after we died, but we probably decomposed into energy, so that death wasn't so bad. In a way, death was life. She used to pull him out of elementary school on whims, make excuses for the grim office ladies—illnesses, doctor and dentist appointments—then take him to museums, the zoo, Disneyland, Knott's Berry Farm, the beach. She told him about erections, wet dreams, condoms, and STDs way before the other kids started talking about these things, warning him that his voice would crack and he'd grow pubic hair, but that the worst part—the part that no one can prepare you for, no school film or sex education class or parent—would be that he'd get his heart shattered and shatter someone else's heart, too. She said to be wary of stupid people so as not to become stupid, because it happens by proximity and osmosis. People love freaks in the movies, she told him, same as me, but it's best to stay away in real life. She said that there were two kinds of people: those who asked why and those who asked what's in it for me, and to avoid the latter because they were dull.

TWO DAYS LATER Ben ditched his second-period world history class. Ditching high school was a new habit, and Nelson was his ditching companion. A sophomore like Ben. A druggie surfer who'd recently lost his father—a plastic surgeon whom he openly admitted to hating—to a heart attack, and whose goal in life was to make headgear and belly-dancing skirts and bikini-like tops from organic hemp and flora for the beautiful women in his future whom he planned to photograph wearing his creations. Nelson smoked pot and tried to get Ben to smoke with him and talked about living in the true glory of the cosmos. Tall, with long, coarse sun-bleached hair and blue eyes, Nelson had a guileless charm sometimes overshadowed by sadness and anger. "Dear Dad," he said, reading aloud to Ben from a letter to his dead father, which he'd apparently written per his therapist's instruction. They both sat on the couch in Nelson's living room. "I miss you." He gave Ben a mischievous anticipatory glance before continuing, "You know your 1957 Mercedes Benz 300SL that cost as much as a house? I'm glad you gave it to Doreen. I didn't want it anyway. Even if you never gave me a fucking thing."

Doreen, Nelson's stepmom, was working out in the family gym—a frantic pulse of music coming from that room—having ignored them when they came inside at 10:15 a.m. on a school day. "Hey, by the way: thanks for the child abuse, Dad," Nelson continued. "It made me who I am. Remember when you shoved me and made me fall against the cabinet? I've got the scar on my head—you know, the one near my ear, seven stitches. Well, thanks, Dad. I'll always remember you, Doctor Fuckhead." He paused, and Ben was tempted to say, Man, that's really sad, but he could tell that wasn't what Nelson wanted, though he had no idea what Nelson did want.

"There's more," Nelson said. "And I drew a picture"—he showed the backside of the paper to Ben: A stick-figure man held a baby, presumably Nelson. There was a heart inside the baby, and the stick-figure dad gripped it with his skeletal hand.

Nelson folded his letter into a tiny square. "Hey," he said, twisting his hips and extending his leg to slip the square inside his jeans pocket. "I googled your mom's disease. Dude," he said in awe. After a pause he repeated and exaggerated the word—"*Dude*"—as in, Are you okay? That's some serious shit.

In a moment of weakness, wanting to keep Nelson's attention,

Ben had told him about his mom and her dog-death request; almost immediately, he'd regretted it. Now Nelson wanted to help with Peanut.

Ben was private about his mother, even breaking up with his girlfriend because of it. He'd been stroking and kissing Tina on his bed one afternoon, his knee between her thighs, hand up her blouse, when his mother called out for him (Rita somewhere outside on a smoke break); by the tone and urgency of her voice, he knew she needed immediate help. Tina sat on his bed waiting while he guided his mother to the toilet, lifted her nightgown, held her steady, and then wiped her ass when she'd finished. The entire time he'd avoided his mom's knowing stare. It felt like Tina was in the bathroom with them. When he went back to his bedroom, Tina's look of compassion sickened him. He decided never to bring anyone to his home again.

THE FOLLOWING AFTERNOON at Nelson's house, Nelson brought up Peanut and how he wanted to help. "I need this," Nelson said, "to prove to myself and to my dad; you know: you're dead, mother-fucker, but watch this."

Ben wouldn't respond, and Nelson watched him over the bong, his mouth sucking at the mouthpiece. He was barefoot and had sloppily painted his toenails and fingernails a slushy purple color, the polish fringing the surrounding skin. He let the smoke out and said, "I'm so sick of your sorry-ass fucking pussy do-nothing loser attitude, you pussy-ass motherfucker. I just want to feel useful. Why don't you trust me?"

Ben got up to leave. Oddly, he wasn't angry. He looked back

before shutting the front door, seeing Nelson's face contorted like he wanted to cry.

BEN WAS RELIEVED to bus tables that evening. His father kept insisting he quit—he gave Ben and his mother plenty of money, after all. But Ben liked work: his emotions manageable with the indifferent customers and the bossy waiters, and the hours eaten away in a comforting dull routine. Sullivan's was a steakhouse with dark wood booths, candlelit, a large bar taking up the side of the restaurant with five giant TVs playing sporting events. His shift passed in a numb reprieve. A long plastic table in the back alleyway beneath a partial awning with a light nestled in the corner was where the employees ate on their breaks. Outside, the wind blew with ocean and Ben noticed the dark storm clouds as he carried a plate of steaming spaghetti with a few forbidden shrimp gifted by the chef hidden under his pasta. He saw Nancy, the hostess, undaunted by the cold weather, her back to the restaurant, a book open at the table, her elbows holding the pages down. Her black hair whipped in the wind, and she wore a man's large green fleece jacket. Ben seated himself opposite, because it would have seemed rude to sit away from her. She began flipping through the book—an intermediate English textbook—but with the wind flapping the pages and his distraction, she gave up and closed it. She looked at him and said, "Community college, to better my English."

"You speak well," he said, and it was true. She spoke English more carefully and thoughtfully than anyone he knew, as if imbuing the words with the meanings they deserved. She also dressed differently from the girls he knew: not so casual, with skirts and dresses and belts and high heels and matching accessories (even hats and gloves). She also wore more makeup: he could see the finish of foundation and powder on her face, her lips lined, and her eyes surrounded by dark blue eyeliner, eyelashes thick—almost pudgy—with mascara.

She took his compliment with a steady look. He knew she'd been Miss Chili Cook-Off a few years past, that she was seventeen, and that she was from Guadalajara, Mexico, but now lived with a man she called Pop Pop and his wife, whom she called Nana, because he'd been at Sullivan's when Pop Pop had introduced her to Billy, their boss—something unsavory about the interaction: Pop Pop a family friend of Nancy's father's, helping her in America, both Billy and Pop Pop standing back to admire her. Why was she named Nancy and not Maria or Teresa or something that sounded Mexican? Pop Pop—fat and pasty, with bulging eyes and a disturbing proprietary air—called Nancy his daughter as if he owned her and was lending her to Billy.

"Aren't you going to eat?" Nancy asked, and he looked down at his plate and saw that the spaghetti wasn't steaming anymore. He'd lost his appetite, a blankness growing inside him. "Wait here," she said, a questioning look on her face. "I'll be right back," and then she was pressing her chair back, rising. She pushed through the door, saying, "Stay," and the door shut behind her.

A piece of paper stuck out from her textbook, and he knew that he had time to take a quick look. He felt his mother urging him to hurry, and he opened the book; saw that she had listed her goals in neat, careful block letters; and read the first two—*send money to family, get good grades*—before shutting the book with a flush of shame. That was his mother infringing, it was something he would not ordinarily do, and he concentrated on the palm trees bending with the wind in the distance, dark against dark. Sprinkles began to wet his hands and arms, bigger drops landing on his head. Nancy returned, holding a glass filled with an unidentifiable food—it looked like streamers coiled inside. "Calamari," she said with a full smile, sitting beside him. She'd pulled her hair into a ponytail. He noticed that the cluster pearl earrings she wore were clip-ons—her ears not pierced—and something about this made him sad, but it was a clear kind of sadness, tender and sure of itself. She handed him the glass and he curled a slippery mesh in the prongs of his fork and then took a bite. She watched him chew, the taste of limes and lettuce and rain—and after he swallowed, he said, "That's really good."

She took her own fork, and this time he watched her. The rain hit them, her hair sticking to her face. He didn't want to leave, but he knew that they would get soaked. "Whoa," she said, looking up at the swirling raindrops, a loud swooshing of wind and rain and palm fronds. She rose, brushing wet hair from her cheek, her expression practical and serious, and then she turned, taking their plates, and he followed her inside.

When he came home, Rita sat at the kitchen table with her nurse shoes crossed underneath the chair, smoking a cigarette, a small plastic ashtray beside a glass of milk. She wasn't supposed to smoke inside, but she'd kept a window open. She ran her cigarette under the tap, washed out her glass and ashtray, set them beside the sink, picked up her paperback novel, and then left by the back door, shutting it gently behind her. He checked on his mother, her body slumped on the sofa bed in the den, Peanut lying next to her, shivering and growling so that he couldn't come closer. He texted Nelson: *I'm ready.*

Not more than fifteen minutes later, Nelson arrived with a cat carrier. He lured a shaky and growling Peanut with a slice of turkey into the carrier, Ben surprised and relieved that he didn't say anything about his mom—didn't even look at her sleeping on the sofa bed, dead to the world via her medications—as if he knew it was nobody's business. Peanut fought, growling and wild, smacking against the sides of the carrier, foam at his mouth. Nelson loaded him into the backseat of his Volkswagen, saying, "I know what I'm doing," but he looked startled, as if trying to convince himself.

At Newport Animal Hospital, Nelson told Ben to wait, but Ben came inside, thinking of his mom and how she wanted him—no one else—to be the one to handle the situation. Nelson had obviously spoken with the woman behind the counter beforehand. Somewhere in her midthirties, she asked no questions. The place was deserted except for her. She had shoulder-length brown hair with dyed splotches of pink and blue near the back. Hair had been tucked behind an ear, and he saw that its entire cartilage was studded with tiny hoops. Peanut slammed against the carrier, yelping and snarling. Ben tried to hand the woman his father's Visa. She wouldn't take it, and he realized she and Nelson had an arrangement. Nelson gave her a wad of cash. When she took a wallet from her purse and placed the bills inside, Ben saw a tiny tattoo on her pointer finger of a skull with fire coming from its mouth. "You don't have to stay," she said, but he told her that he did. They followed her to an examination room, Nelson carrying the carrier. After several tries she was able to muzzle

Peanut, and they held the dog while she sedated him. She wore blue latex gloves, and Ben was glad her tattoo was covered. Peanut lay on the steel examining table, his tail between his legs, and gave Ben a tolerant half-lidded stare. As she inserted the needle and injected the dog, she assured them that Peanut wasn't feeling pain. Ben saw the prick of blood at his fur when she pulled the needle from his leg. They watched for several minutes until Peanut's rib cage stilled, each of them petting the dog and murmuring comforting words. Ben heard himself say, "Good dog; it's okay. You're a good boy." He felt woozy and very sad. The woman, closing Peanut's eyelids with her blue-gloved fingertips, asked if Ben needed to be alone to say goodbye. He said that he did not. Before they left, she offered them hot chocolates from a pot of hot water and a basket of tea bags and Swiss Miss packets by the coffeemaker. "No thanks," Ben said. He followed Nelson's figure in the dark to the Volkswagen, and when Nelson opened the passenger door for him, he felt their friendship sinking into a deeper silent realm.

THE NEXT MORNING, Ben woke with a start. When he entered the den, Sharon—the Monday-Wednesday-Friday caretaker— was lifting his mother by her underarms to slide her into Tara. Sharon leaned over with her back to him to arrange his mother's legs in the wheelchair and said, "Peanut's gone. Must've gotten out," and his mother stared at him over Sharon's back, her eyes blazing.

•

THAT SAME WEEK his father called, and they had a long phone conversation. He'd found out about Ben's absences but wasn't going to punish him—at least not yet. As he talked on about college and Ben's future, it occurred to Ben how lonely his father was, and that his mother had probably asked him to leave, his love blooming helplessly with her illness and rejection. He felt protective and vowed to do better. He thought of Nelson's stick-figure dad snatching the heart from the baby Nelson. His mother seemed to be disconnecting lately: averting her fierce eyes, letting him out of her stare, as if shielding him, passing him over to his father, to Nelson, to Nancy, to whoever else might care for him—folding herself away, like Nelson's little square of paper. Soon, she'd fold herself so tight that, as in a magic trick, she'd disappear. But he knew that was impossible.

LATER THAT AFTERNOON Nancy invited him over, since Pop Pop and Nana weren't home. Earlier they'd gone to the beach and swum in the surf. She'd worn a conservative black one-piece, cut low at her thighs and high at her chest. He'd looked away when she'd toweled off. She'd told him that her family had money, and that she was only staying with Pop Pop and Nana for a vacation. He didn't believe her. She said that she'd heard his mom was very sick, but she didn't press him on the subject. He liked how she made words seem like something else, something completely her own, when she mispronounced them.

Her bedroom was how he'd imagined it: beige walls with framed paintings of sunflowers and daisies, a skirted and mirrored vanity table with perfumes and makeup and a thick-bristled hairbrush with a comb stuck in the middle. In other words, a room that would never quite be hers, but Nana and Pop Pop's guest room with Nancy living in it. He was pleased to be with her. Everything seemed unreal, and he was both sheltered and floating in anticipation, reminding him of his mother's intimacy: limitless, close, constant, unknown.

Nancy opened a window, set the curtain back so that they could see the side of another house, a hedge and a water heater. He sat on her bed. It had a dust ruffle and so many fat pillows that she had to put them on the floor so that they had space to sit. As she settled beside him—kicking off her shoes—he watched her thighs and heard them brush against each other. She folded her legs beneath her, and he was surprised, having not seen a young woman wearing pantyhose before, a darker seam at her toes.

"I lied," she said, "about my family. I don't know why." She looked disappointed and concerned.

"I do things all the time," he said, hoping to make her feel better, "that I don't understand."

"I miss them," she said.

"I miss my mom," he said, "and I live with her."

She nodded.

"Will you go back?" he asked, and when she didn't answer, he said, "Can't you leave?" As he watched her, he understood that her situation—like his own—was far more complicated than it seemed.

She took his hand and pressed it into the bed. He let himself slide into sensation, moving closer, leaning so that his mouth touched her hair, and then he heard her whisper, "No, no. I can't go home."

Acknowledgments

My love and gratitude to Michelle Huneven, Dana Johnson, Danzy Senna, and Sarah Shun-lien Bynum: my stories are better for your insights and wisdom, and your friendships sustain me.

Thank you, Michael Carlisle, Jack Shoemaker, and Jane Vandenburgh for your love and loyalty. I'm so grateful. Thank you also to Megan Fishmann, Dan Smetanka, and everyone at Counterpoint.

I also want to thank the literary journals where these stories originally appeared, and especially the *Santa Monica Review* and Andrew Tonkovich, literary brother extraordinaire. Your support means so much to me.

As always, Chris, Cole, and Ry.

Permissions Acknowledgments

The following stories first appeared in these publications:

"Appetite" originally appeared in *Zyzzyva: A San Francisco Journal of Arts and Letters*, Summer 2017.

"Confetti" originally appeared as "Small Dreams" in slightly different form in *The Rattling Wall* 5 (2015).

"DC" originally appeared in slightly different form in *Santa Monica Review*, Spring 2018.

"Dogs" originally appeared in slightly different form in *Santa Monica Review*, Fall 2012.

"Half-Truth" originally appeared in slightly different form in *Slake: Los Angeles* 2 (2011); and in Patricia O'Sullivan, ed., *Literary Pasadena: The Fiction Edition* (Altadena, CA: Prospect Park Books, 2013).

"Johnny Hitman" originally appeared in slightly different form in *Santa Monica Review*, Twentieth Anniversary Edition, Spring 2008; and also as a notable mention in Alice Sebold, ed., *The Best American Stories: 2009* (New York: Mariner Books, 2009).

"Nobody's Business" originally appeared in slightly different form in *Alaska Quarterly Review* 27, nos. 3 and 4 (Fall/Winter 2010).

"Parking Far Away" originally appeared in *Crate Literary Magazine: Monsters & Villains*, Spring 2006.

"Vandals" originally appeared in slightly different form in *Juxta-Prose* 14 (December 2017).

"We Know Things" originally appeared in slightly different form in *Santa Monica Review*, Fall 2014.

Author photograph © Gabriel Mason

VICTORIA PATTERSON is the author of the novels *The Little Brother*, *The Peerless Four*, and *This Vacant Paradise*, a 2011 *New York Times Book Review* Editors' Choice. She lives in South Pasadena, California, with her family and teaches at Antioch University. Find more at victoriapatterson.com.